"Have you ever been in love?"

Judith stared at him openmouthed. A slow flush crawled up her face. "That's a very personal question. Why the interest in my private life?"

"Just curious," Luke shrugged, looking oddly confused as though he wasn't sure himself why he was quizzing her. "People like you are locked safes. I just wondered if there was a combination that would open you up."

"Do your safecracking elsewhere," said Judith, moving with purpose toward the door.

Luke took hold of her wrists and began to pull her to him. Judith wanted to feel his mouth on her own, but she reminded herself that he was engaged to Baba. She was furious with herself.

"I'd better go," she muttered, pulling away with an effort of willpower.

Books by Charlotte Lamb

A VIOLATION

HARLEQUIN PRESENTS

387—THE CRUEL FLAME
393—OBSESSION
401—SAVAGE SURRENDER
404—NIGHT MUSIC
412—MAN'S WORLD
417—STRANGER IN THE NIGHT
422—COMPULSION
428—SEDUCTION
435—ABDUCTION
442—RETRIBUTION
448—ILLUSION
451—CRESCENDO
460—HEARTBREAKER
466—DANGEROUS
472—DESIRE
478—THE GIRL FROM NOWHERE
528—MIDNIGHT LOVER
545—A WILD AFFAIR
585—BETRAYAL
635—THE SEX WAR
644—HAUNTED
658—A SECRET INTIMACY
668—DARKNESS OF THE HEART
700—INFATUATION

HARLEQUIN ROMANCES

2083—FESTIVAL SUMMER
2103—FLORENTINE SPRING
2161—HAWK IN A BLUE SKY
2181—MASTER OF COMUS
2206—DESERT BARBARIAN

These books may be available at your local bookseller.

For a free catalog listing all titles currently available, send your name and address to:

Harlequin Reader Service
P.O. Box 52040, Phoenix, AZ 85072-2040
Canadian address: Stratford, Ontario N5A 6W2

CHARLOTTE LAMB

infatuation

Harlequin Books

TORONTO • NEW YORK • LONDON
AMSTERDAM • PARIS • SYDNEY • HAMBURG
STOCKHOLM • ATHENS • TOKYO • MILAN

Harlequin Presents first edition June 1984
ISBN 0-373-10700-5

Original hardcover edition published in 1984
by Mills & Boon Limited

CHAPTER ONE

JUDITH walked back to her office through Central Park; she was going to be late, but she couldn't force herself to hurry. She had had a very good lunch with some delicious wine which still circulated in her veins and it was one of those days in late autumn when New York shimmers in an elegiac sunlight. She watched the golden trees overhead; their leaves had suddenly begun to crisp and curl, rustling like banknotes in the counting wind which occasionally peeled one off and sent it whirling along the avenues and walks where lovers sat looking dreamily at each other and men in city suits furtively ate sandwiches from silver foil wrappers, scattering the crumbs for pigeons whose grey plumage was iridescent in the sunshine. Any day now the trees would be bare, shivering; the snow would come floating down the canyons of Manhattan and Judith would have to scurry out of the office into the subway without so much as a glance at the park. She might as well, she felt, enjoy today while she could.

As she finally reached the Schewitz and Quayle building she looked at her watch, shrugging. Half an hour late. Well, John wasn't likely to say too much; she was usually very punctual. She produced her security card for the uniformed porter who was already waving her past into the shadowy foyer.

'I know who *you* are, Miss Murry,' he said with a grin.

'I might have a bomb in my handbag,' Judith told him gravely, and he laughed.

'Oh, I can't see you blowing the old place up,' he said, looking around the foyer.

'Can't you?' Judith walked towards the lift before he could answer that. She went up to the fourth floor and stepped out of the lift, expecting the usual sepulchral hush, only to take two steps towards her office and halt in disbelief. What on earth was happening in the conference room? It sounded like someone shouting. She couldn't believe her ears. It was one of the unwritten rules in the bank that voices were never raised. If you are going bankrupt do it quietly and don't do it here, the board's attitude suggested.

She stood outside the great carved walnut doors of the conference room, feeling rather like a parlourmaid listening at a keyhole, except that she didn't have to stoop to hear the crash of someone's fist on the long, polished table inside.

'Get that and get it good. It isn't over, you can take it from me. I'll wipe the smiles off your faces!'

The door opened before Judith could get out of the way and a man came through it so fast that he almost knocked her over. He paused long enough to give her a glare from hard grey eyes and to yell over his shoulder to the men hurrying after him: 'Even the office furniture here tries to trip you up!' then he stalked off, with a huddle of men in well-tailored grey suits bleating in his wake like worried sheep. They weren't men she knew, any more than their leader was; Judith glared after them. Office furniture? Charming. Who on earth was he? She glanced through the open door of the room he had left and saw the board sitting around the table in what seemed to be a shell-shocked silence. She hadn't had time to catch more than a glimpse of the man with grey eyes who had now vanished into the lift, but she had been left with an indelible impression of height and power, so she wasn't surprised by seeing alarm in the faces of the men he had just been bellowing at.

'Where on earth have you been, Judith?' The voice

made her turn, still bemused. She smiled at her boss wryly.

'Sorry, I know I'm late, but lunch dragged on and on, I couldn't get away.'

'Anything come out of it?' John asked, falling into step beside her as they moved towards Judith's office.

'The Wiener Schnitzel was delicious, and they served a very good Riesling with it.' She had been lunching with a stockbroker of impeccable manners and passable good looks. Trying to get him to see a joke, however, was like trying to borrow money when you need it— practically impossible, unless you have a gun in your hand. She had been very disappointed; his first appearance hadn't revealed his feet of clay, she had had high hopes of him for a while.

John laughed a little blankly. 'I often wonder what you're talking about.'

'Don't worry, I ask myself the same thing. John, who on earth was that who just hurtled out of the conference room? I don't like to sound alarmist, but I think he was shouting and he certainly seemed to be in a hurry. Wall Street didn't just crash again, did it?'

John looked a little nervously over his shoulder at this blasphemy. 'That was Luke Doulton. We've been putting together a take-over bid for one of his companies and he wasn't very happy about it.' He looked disapproving. 'Rather foolish of him to get so upset. There's nothing he can do about it now; we've been successful, he might as well accept it like a gentleman.'

'He didn't *look* much like a gentleman,' Judith said thoughtfully, remembering those angry grey eyes. 'In fact, he looked as mad as hell.'

'Judith, please ... it upsets the chairman if he hears women swear.' John pushed open her office door and she walked past him, smiling. 'We've only just managed to persuade him that women can do more than file a letter or take shorthand. Remember how old he is . . .'

'I remember it every day,' said Judith, shedding her camelhair jacket and sitting down behind her desk. She swivelled in her black leather chair, studying John. 'Luke Doulton . . . that must be Doulton-Klein.'

'Doulton-Klein International,' John corrected; he was always insistent on total accuracy. They had worked together now for six years, there wasn't much she did not know about John. Although, she thought, watching him, perhaps she was wrong about him; nobody could be as easy to read as that, John must hide something from her. Who knew what dark secrets he had? Perhaps he grew begonias in his New York apartment or had a passion for eating blueberry pie in bed, or went birdwatching on Sunday mornings in the park before New York woke up. Whenever she met someone who seemed transparent and dull she amused herself with inventing bizarre secret tastes or sinister backgrounds for them. She met a lot of very dull people; she had to pass the time somehow.

John was talking when she surfaced again. 'His father was the brains of the outfit—the son took over a going concern.'

'If I remember their quotation of this morning they haven't exactly gone downhill since,' Judith said drily, and John laughed.

'They haven't, no! And you never forget a share price, so don't pretend you can't remember theirs. Luke Doulton is a very clever guy.'

'That was my impression. I hope we haven't bitten off more than we can chew,' said Judith. 'Mr Doulton didn't look to me like a man who lets go of anything he owns without a fight.'

John looked worried, and so, within twenty-four hours, did the members of the board as they realised that they had somehow made a mistake. Luke Doulton had defeated their take-over bid and was firmly back in control of his company, adding another legend to those which already clung around his name. The company who had retained the bank to secure the take-over retreated morosely, very displeased with the bank's handling of the affair, and Judith made an addition to her mental file of people who would bear watching. Luke Doulton was certainly one of them. He was, she discovered, almost a mythical figure in the Wall Street world; although he was still in his thirties he had never lost a boardroom battle. His father had been a giant in the world of international finance; gathering together in a very short time a vast empire made up of many different companies in many different countries. When he died everyone had leapt to the conclusion that his empire was up for grabs. Nobody had expected the son to be able to control the corporation, but they had had to admit that they were wrong before a year had passed. After a short power struggle with the ambitious, ruthless men surrounding him Luke Doulton had emerged the winner, and he had stayed firmly in control ever since.

'Very shrewd of you to guess that Doulton would beat us off,' said John with a mixture of congratulation and wariness over lunch a week later in the 21 Club. They were waiting for a client from Hong Kong who had asked if they could eat at the legendary restaurant. He was late; they were sipping very dry Martinis and watching the other guests filtering past under the watchful eye of the security guards on the door. 'But your guesswork is often inspired, I don't know how you do it. I thought we had Doulton tied hand and foot.'

'He didn't look like a man who stays tied up for long,' said Judith. 'This Martini is much too strong; one more of these and I'll be floating a few feet above the sidewalk!'

John laughed and Judith watched, suddenly alert, as she saw Luke Doulton coming towards them. The head waiter was practically sweeping the carpet in front of him. Judith glanced from Luke Doulton's hard-edged face to that of the girl with him; she was very pretty and had decided that autumn was the right season for mink. It looked good on her and she looked good on Luke Doulton's arm, which was no doubt why she was there. Judith had an idea he would always choose luxury items like this swaying, expensive redhead.

'No, no, I'll keep my coat on—I'm cold,' the girl said to a waiter who unkindly tried to dispossess her of the mink, and fluttered her lashes at the man to whose arm she clung.

'The pheasant is particularly good today, Mr Doulton, just the way you like it,' the head waiter murmured.

Judith was enjoying the passing show when it halted in front of her and John; who almost spilled his Martini in his haste to rise.

'Don't get up, I wouldn't want to disturb you,' Luke Doulton said, but the advice was given too late; John already looked disturbed. He sank back, though, clutching his glass and forcing a worried smile.

'And how are all my friends at Schewitz and Quayle?' Luke Doulton asked pleasantly.

'Oh, fine, sir, thank you,' John stammered, looking even more unhappy over this kind question.

'That's good,' said Luke Doulton. 'I always remember my friends.' And never forget my enemies, his grey eyes added silently, then they moved from their study of John to glance over Judith, less with interest than with what she suspected to be curiosity about John's taste in women. She knew she wasn't going to be any competition for his lady friend; she didn't have a mink and her cream dress was very simple and businesslike—but then she was here to work, not decorate the view. Luke Doulton's gaze eventually reached her face after a thoughtful tour of the rest of her and she stared back at him coolly. John misunderstood his inspection and began to stammer an introduction: 'Mr Doulton, this is . . .'

He never finished the sentence. Luke Doulton had given him a nod and walked off before he could get Judith's name out.

John's voice tailed away, he drank some more of his Martini, very flushed. 'That was terrible—I didn't know what to say to him. He's a very alarming man.'

'I hope the pheasant is over-ripe!' Judith muttered with ferocity, and John stared at her blankly.

'The pheasant? Judith, what are you talking about?'

'Get your smile back—here comes the client,' she said under her breath as she recognised the man coming down the stairs.

They ate half an hour later in the dark oak-panelled room hung with sporting prints; there were very few women there. Judith could hear the soft giggling of the girl with Luke Doulton, she could almost swear she picked up her perfume, although they were several tables away. John was doing most of the talking, only bringing Judith in when the subject touched on her own expertise with the international market; for minutes at a time she could let her attention wander without danger, and she found herself watching Luke Doulton and his companion, wondering what they were talking about. Not the stock market, that was for sure, she decided; the redhead didn't look as if she knew a bull market from a bear. If figures were under discussion they would not be company accounts. She saw Luke Doulton touch his champagne glass to that of the girl, who slipped a red rose from the vase on the table and kissed it before trailing it across his mouth. Oh, very pretty, Judith thought, if this is how they go on at lunchtime I wonder where they've got to by dinner? Will he go back to his office afterwards, or is this a prelude to more private business?

As she and John left an hour later she heard some woman in the foyer say: 'Did you see who was there today? Luke Doulton ... I must say, he's a very charming man.'

'And so good-looking,' her friend agreed.

'Excuse me,' Judith said coldly. She did not think Luke Doulton was charming; he had turned his back and walked away when John began to introduce her, that was no indication of charm. He was a very wealthy man; no doubt he didn't feel he had any need to be polite, especially as she was neither particularly pretty nor very chic. He had probably assessed her clothes and done so accurately; from the stories she had heard about him he was accustomed to paying for haute couture clothes for his lady friends, so he could probably price your every garment at a glance. He was very attractive himself and his companion had obviously thought he was a walking dream, but Judith had decided she did not like him.

She went back to the bank with John and buried herself in a study of the latest movements on the Hong Kong exchange. By the time she went back to her apartment that evening she had forgotten all about Luke Doulton and his bad manners, and he did not crop up again over the following weeks as winter tightened its grip on the city and her life narrowed down to a long day at the bank followed by a gruelling trip home and quiet evening. She was very busy that winter; she had no time to go to the theatre very often and her love life was rather dull. She was dating a computer expert with a passion for taping odd noises like the whine of a kettle or the sound of a jet over the city, then mixing them with classical music or jazz. He was rather good-looking and could be lively at a party or when they were out at dinner, but once he was back in his own apartment he lost all interest in everything but his hobby. After several months of this Judith gave up the unequal struggle. She could not go on taking second place to a whistling kettle.

The last of the snow was just turning to sludge on the New York pavements when she got a phone call in the middle of one chilly night. Her grandfather had died in London. She flew home later that day, coolly working out as she sat on the plane that she was going to have to leave New York for good. She couldn't live on one side of the Atlantic while her grandmother was alone on the other side.

After the funeral she flew back to New York, but merely to wind up her affairs; give in her notice to Schewitz and Quayle, pack up all her possessions and arrange for those she wanted to keep to be shipped to England, and sublet her apartment for the rest of her very expensive lease. That had been the easiest part of leaving New York. Apartments were like gold dust; she had been overwhelmed with eager apartment-hunters from the minute she contacted an agency.

Spring had definitely arrived when she got back to London; within a few days the trees had come into fat, sticky bud and green leaves showed everywhere. Judith was staying with her grandmother for the moment. Mrs Murry seemed to her to have shrunk over the past few years; as light as a child and very thin, only her silvery hair and lined skin betrayed that she was seventy, a fact she would otherwise have denied and certainly resented. She refused to behave as though she was old and she kept trying to persuade Judith to go back to New York.

'I'm not helpless, you know. Don't worry about me. Good heavens, anyone would think I was a child!' she protested.

'I'm not going back to New York unless you come with me—and you know you wouldn't leave this house. We're not going to have another long argument, are we? I'm in a hurry, I'm going to have lunch with Ruth.' They had been arguing for weeks, ever since the funeral. Mrs Murry might be small and frail but she was incredibly stubborn. She never gave up on a fight, but Judith was her flesh and blood, she had the same obstinacy and determination.

Sulkily Mrs Murry said: 'Give my love to Ruth and the children,' and Judith left to catch her bus. It was a fine April day; the sky impossibly blue and the air fresh and sweet. In that brilliant light London's ancient familiarity had a novelty which surprised. Judith absorbed what she saw with pleasure while her mind was preoccupied with more mundane thoughts. Sooner or later, and probably sooner because she was going to need the money, she was going to have to get another job. She could go back to the London office of Schewitz and Quayle, of course, but she had been quite high on the career ladder in New York; doing a highly responsible and demanding job and earning a very good salary. She might not get an equivalent offer here.

In many ways she regretted the sudden break in her career. She had enjoyed working in New York; she liked the people she worked with, was fascinated by the job she did and loved the city itself. If it had not been for her grandfather's death she wouldn't have thought of coming back.

She couldn't discuss any of this with Mrs Murry, who would merely urge her to go back to New York. In spite of her grandmother's protests Judith suspected that Mrs Murry was relieved to have her back home;

she simply did not want to admit it, she did not want to feel she was pushing Judith into staying. Mrs Murry was prickly and independent, but Judith wanted to be on hand whenever her grandmother needed her. When she was a child, her grandmother had always been there when Judith needed *her*.

Judith's father had died when she was six and his wife and child had gone to live with his parents. Her mother had got a job and left Judith with Mrs Murry during the day. When Judith was fourteen her mother had married again. Judith had never liked her stepfather much; he wasn't unkind to her, merely indifferent, especially after her mother had given birth to his two sons. He had taken them all to America and Judith had felt an outsider in the little family. She had worked hard at school to compensate for her increasing isolation at home; too worried and miserable to make many friends, she had grown increasingly homesick, too. She longed for her grandparents, for London and everything she had grown up with, and as soon as she had left school she had come back to live with her grandparents, getting a job in a London bank. At the time it had been the only offer made to her, she hadn't intended at that stage to make a career in banking, but when she was twenty-three her boss had been transferred to the New York office and had asked Judith to go with him. She had decided it would be good for her career to accept and had rapidly risen in the firm, moving up whenever her boss did. She would miss John Atkins; there had never been any romantic tinge to their relationship, but they had been firm friends and trusted each other. John wasn't the marrying kind; he was too set on becoming a very big wheel in international banking.

'You can't be serious! You're throwing away a marvellous career!' he had protested when she resigned, and she had known he was right, but some things were

more important than careers. Whatever her grandmother pretended, her life was going to be very lonely
now and Judith was not going to leave her in London
without a relative in the world.

The bus pulled up with a jerk and she suddenly
realised she had reached her destination, so she leapt up
and sprinted to the stairs, taking them two at a time.

'Hey, miss, you can't jump off when we're going!'
The bus conductor swung towards her and she grinned
at him as she jumped. She landed lightly and waved,
and he scowled back at her, his cap tilted back on his
head.

The only friend from her schooldays with whom she
had kept in touch had been a girl whose parents lived
across the road from the Murry house. Ruth had got
married when she was twenty-one and Judith had been
one of her bridesmaids. The other had been Ruth's
younger sister, Barbara. They had hardly been a
matching pair. Judith had looked gloomily at Barbara
as they both stood in front of the mirror on that
wedding morning. She had been tempted to refuse to go
through with it; people would smile behind their hands
as she and Baba walked behind Ruth.

Judith was slightly built, fine-boned, sallow-skinned
and straight-haired; with slanting dark eyes which
mostly looked down because at that age she was very
shy, a mouth which was slightly too large and a small,
snub nose. Her figure was like a boy's; breasts tiny, hips
narrow, legs skinny. She was grateful if she passed
unnoticed; it had made her face burn to hear people
say: she's so *plain*! Neither Ruth nor Barbara were ever
called plain. Ruth was small and cuddly and curly-
haired and had a smile like the sun rising. She was kind
and warm and cheerful, from the age of fourteen she
had boys queueing up to take her out, and her
confidence attracted people while Judith's shyness made

them avoid her. Judith did not mind the fact that Ruth was so popular because Ruth was her best friend and she was fond of her, but Barbara was another kettle of fish. Barbara was beautiful. In Ruth's company, Judith was never aware of her own appearance—when she was with Barbara, she *felt* plain.

Not that Baba went out of her way to stress the difference between them. Baba wasn't malicious, there wasn't a spiteful bone in her body, it wasn't her fault that she was so ravishing that people stared and gasped when she walked past. She had great soft masses of honey-blonde curls, wide-open baby blue eyes and a perfectly shaped pink mouth. Her figure was all curves; full, high breasts, a small waist, smoothly rounded hips and long, shapely legs. When she was a little girl, Ruth used to call her Shirley Temple, and in many ways that was exactly her image; sunny-tempered and sweet-natured and full of vitality. Baba was amazingly old-fashioned, too. Any man who took her out imagining that he would get her into bed soon discovered his mistake, and retired with a slapped face. Her parents adored her, she should have been totally spoilt, but she had grown up without altering very much. At twenty-one she was almost the same girl she had been at twelve, in spite of having been a fashion model for three years. In every way, Baba was amazing, but she still made Judith feel plain.

That was precisely how she felt now as Baba opened the front door of Ruth's house; her figure tightly encased in white jeans and a silky black top with a very low neckline. Giving Judith a glowing smile, she said: 'Hallo, how are you? Ages since I saw you—you look wonderful, so brown!'

'You look fabulous yourself,' said Judith with rather more honesty. She had not seen Baba since she got back from the States. Ruth had come to her grandfather's funeral and they had talked for a while afterwards. When Judith got back from settling her affairs in New York, she had rung Ruth and been invited over for lunch, but Ruth had not mentioned that Baba would be there.

'Come on in; everyone's in the garden,' said Baba, and swayed off along the narrow hall on ludicrously high heels. 'I'm sorry about your grandfather; he was a darling, I was very fond of him. How's your grandmother bearing up?'

'She misses him, but she won't show it.' Judith sometimes wished her grandmother was not quite so independent, but she admired her for her strength of will. 'Are you having lunch with us, Baba? How's the modelling going? Still very successful?' She had seen a woman's magazine cover from which Baba's face stared out only that morning, so obviously Baba's career was still rising.

'Oh, there's lots to tell,' Baba said, and threw her another of those too-beautiful smiles; they never quite seemed real, any more than Baba did, anything approaching perfection is somehow uncomfortable. Judith had often wished she could dislike Baba, it would make it easier to bear those amazing looks, but Baba had persistently refused to do or say anything to make it possible, which, in itself, was maddening.

'I might be going to make a film,' Baba told her.

'Good heavens,' Judith murmured, wishing she could sound more incredulous and awed but hardly even surprised. The only thing which would really amaze her about Baba was if she ran off with the milkman or went bald. Good luck was something which had rained relentlessly into Baba's lap, for as long as Judith had known her.

'In Hollywood,' Baba added.

'Where else?' Judith said almost wearily. 'What sort of film is it?'

'It's about a model—it's that book, you know, the best-seller everyone was reading last year. It isn't settled yet; we're waiting to hear if I've got the part. The director has been auditioning hundreds of girls, but my agent says he's very keen on me.' Baba halted on the little patio at the back of the house and gave a deep sigh, giving Judith one of her wide-eyed looks. 'But even if they offer it to me I don't know if I could bear to go.'

Ruth had got up from the lounger on which she had been sunbathing, taking off her sunglasses and dropping them on to the book beside the goldfish pool. She came over to hug Judith warmly. 'You're looking better than you did at the funeral. How's Mrs Murry? Why didn't you bring her with you? I was expecting her.'

'She isn't up to talking to people yet, but she sent you a message—her love and she hopes you'll come over soon and bring the children.' Judith glanced towards them and smiled. They were perched on the rim of the goldfish pond, dragging shrimping nets through the lily leaves. 'I don't recognise them!' she said, and Ruth laughed.

'Of course you don't—when you were home last, Stevie was in his pram and Julie was just starting to walk.' Ruth pulled the nearest child down and swivelled her to face Judith. 'Say hello to Auntie Judith.'

Julie stared, her thumb going into her mouth. Ruth pulled it out. Julie went on staring and didn't say anything. Ruth lifted the little boy down but could not persuade him to relinquish his net which he trailed thoughtfully across Judith's feet, leaving a fragment of green weed on her shoe. 'Little beast,' Ruth congratulated him. 'They do talk, although you might not believe it. In a couple of hours you'll wish they didn't!'

'That sun's quite hot, isn't it?' observed Baba,

unzipping her jeans. Judith watched in surprise as Baba pulled off her clothes, under which, it turned out, she was wearing a skimpy bikini. Her skin had the perfect lustre of polished gold. She lay down gracefully on one of the loungers and closed her eyes. Stevie went over to stare at her.

'Come and help me get the lunch,' Ruth said to Judith. 'Salad, I thought; okay?'

'Fine,' said Judith, watching Stevie as he dipped his net in the pool and then delicately sprinkled Baba with water. Without opening her eyes, Baba said: 'Don't do that, Stevie, there's a good boy.'

'If you can't behave yourself with those nets I'll have to lock them away,' Ruth told her offspring, who retreated to the far side of the pool and started fishing for lily pads again.

Judith followed Ruth back into the house. Ruth had put on weight, she was rounder and more curvy than she had been, and she had cut her hair short without persuading it to uncurl so that her head was covered with tight, fat little coils of goldy brown.

'Marriage appears to agree with you—how's David?' Judith asked her.

Ruth smiled. 'He's fine; still very busy at the agency.' David ran an estate agent's office in Hampstead and was very successful at it, judging by the elegant little house he had acquired for his family. He was nearly ten years older than Ruth, a quiet, thoughtful man with a thin, wiry figure and dark brown hair.

'Did Baba tell you her news?' asked Ruth as she got a large bowl of prepared salad out of the fridge.

'About the possible film? Yes, she was just telling me . . .'

'Oh, not that,' said Ruth. 'Her engagement.'

Judith had begun making the dressing for the salad; she stopped, mid-whisk, to stare. 'Engagement? She

never breathed a word—when did this happen? Who is
he?'

Ruth laughed. 'Don't let that curdle, will you?'

'Sorry,' said Judith, smiling back and concentrated
on her whisking. Ruth was working at her elbow,
slicing hard-boiled eggs and dicing cheese, her movements swift and efficient, but talking quickly as she
worked.

'It isn't official yet, they haven't bought the ring,
they're going to do that this afternoon and it will be
announced in *The Times* tomorrow.'

'The lucky man has money, I gather,' Judith said
drily, and Ruth gave her a sideways look.

'That must be the understatement of the year! Guess
who she's marrying; you may well know him—I bet you
know him, his name has got to be familiar to you, of all
people.'

Judith's fine dark brows lifted. 'How intriguing—I
don't know that many rich men except clients in New
York . . .' Her voice broke off as Ruth smiled. 'He's
American?'

'Uh-huh.'

'Heavens! Even so, that still leaves the field wide
open—you're going to have to tell me, we could go on
playing guessing games all night.'

'Spoilsport,' Ruth laughed, then paused. 'Luke
Doulton!' Her voice held a ring of what was
undoubtedly triumph and glee in what she expected
Judith's reaction to be—and she was not disappointed.
Judith looked at her in stunned amazement.

'*The* Luke Doulton?'

'Is there more than one?'

'You mean the Luke Doulton who runs Doulton-
Klein International?' Judith couldn't believe her ears.
She had long ago given up hope that Baba would do
anything to surprise her, anything had always seemed

possible with someone as lucky and beautiful as Baba, but now, at last, Baba had succeeded. The last man in the world Judith would ever have imagined falling for Baba was Luke Doulton. It didn't surprise, of course, that he had entered Baba's life; he had entered the lives of a great many beautiful girls, if rumour was to be believed, and exited again with only a very brief stop in between. Baba was a well-known international model who liked jet-set life; sooner or later she had been bound to run into Luke Doulton, and with his reputation it must have been on the cards that he would date her for a while—but that he might actually ask her to marry him was a possibility on which no sane bookmaker interested in staying in business would have taken a bet.

'Shut your mouth, love, you look daft,' said Ruth, laughing.

'I'm stunned!'

'You look it. Do you know him? I wondered if you might have met him in New York. Baba said she mentioned you to him but he didn't know your name.'

'No, he wouldn't,' Judith said drily. He might have done if he had allowed John to finish introducing her, but she had been beneath the level at which he noticed people. 'Men like Luke Doulton don't hobnob with ordinary bank staff,' she told Ruth. 'How did Baba meet him?'

'At a party in Hawaii, of all places. Baba was modelling over there and someone introduced them. Apparently it was love at first sight; isn't it romantic? It was a whirlwind romance; he followed her to New York and proposed. They've only known each other a month.' Ruth laughed excitedly, washing her hands at the sink as she talked. 'I can hardly believe it myself, but Baba's taking it very calmly. He's terribly rich, you know.'

'Yes,' said Judith. 'That's a very slippery fish Baba has caught; hundreds of others have tried to net him and failed.' How odd that Baba hadn't mentioned her engagement, she thought. She had burst out with the news about the possible film but hadn't breathed a word about Luke Doulton—but then perhaps she thought Judith already knew about it?

Ruth looked worried as she started loading a tray with the food. 'You don't think he isn't serious? Oh, dear, Baba would be so upset. When we were kids I often used to wish she would do something nasty—just to prove she was human, you know. I'd pull her hair or pinch her, I thought she'd run and tell tales, but she never did—she used to go and cry in a corner and make me ashamed of myself. It was maddening!'

'Poor Ruth,' said Judith, amused. 'She must have been a drag to live with.'

'She was—I've felt terribly sorry for Cinderella's elder sisters ever since.' Ruth walked to the door with one tray and Judith followed with the other, smiling.

Baba was still lying on the lounger, the sunlight turning her hair to drifting clouds of gold, making her perfectly proportioned body shimmer; she was so totally relaxed that you felt her head must be quite empty.

'Food,' Ruth said decisively. Baba sat up and the children swarmed around the table complaining about the food.

'Ugh, rabbits' food,' groaned Stevie as he crammed his mouth, and his mother said sharply: 'Don't put so much in your mouth, you already look like a hamster.'

'Ruth told me about your engagement,' Judith said to Baba. 'I hope you'll be very happy.'

Baba gave her a glowing smile. 'Oh, thank you, Judith; you are sweet. What are you going to do now that you're back in London? Have you got another job yet?'

'I'm looking around,' Judith said evasively.

'Will you live with your grandmother?'

'She's far too independent, to want me around all day. I'm looking for a flat within easy reach of her house.' She picked up a small square of cheese and studied it wryly. 'Not much to ask, really—a good job and a flat.'

Baba laughed and said: 'You must come to our engagement party; Luke's in banking, too. We're getting engaged today, he's coming to pick me up at three and take me to choose a ring. Luke's planning a big party at the Savoy, there'll be masses of people there, I'll get Luke to introduce you to some useful people in banking, you might be offered a new job.'

'Thank you,' said Judith with what she considered extreme restraint. Along with a number of other characteristics she had inherited her grandmother's prickly independence and dislike of being patronised or offered pity; she felt, in any case, that she was in no need of either from Baba. While she was in New York she had had plenty of boy-friends; she just hadn't felt she couldn't live without any of them. They were all nice, she enjoyed their company, but none of them had touched her heart. Several times she had thought briefly: this is it, this is him, but it never had been, it had only been a momentary impulse, a romantic glow brought on by moonlight, one glass of champagne too many or her own dreamy desire to be swept off her feet. The next second she would notice that his ears were too big or he only talked about profit and loss or that he was quite obviously the biggest bore in Manhattan, which explained why, looking like a younger version of Robert Redford, he was still running around loose. Judith had a private theory that when love did come it would be because in spite of all such drawbacks the guy in question would be for some reason totally irresistible and someone you could happily face at breakfast for thirty years. Until such a man appeared on the horizon she refused to compromise or accept anything less.

Baba studied her thoughtfully. 'Luke knows simply everybody, I'll have a word with him about you.'

'Please don't,' Judith said tersely; remembering all too vividly the last time she had met him.

'It's no bother.' Baba gave her a ravishing smile, blind to her irritation.

Judith decided not to get into a long wrangle about it; no doubt Baba would soon find out that the formidable Luke Doulton, however crazy about her at the moment, was not going to take on unknown females just to please her. He would probably say: tell this friend to get in touch with me. Then Judith could safely ignore the whole thing. One thing was certain—no way was she going to allow herself to be put in such an invidious position, nobody would ever believe she had any ability if her job was handed to her on a plate by Luke Doulton's future wife. She would never live it down. Everyone she worked with would watch her suspiciously, waiting for her to betray her inadequacy. She couldn't blame them, either. After all, if she was good enough why shouldn't she get a job purely on her own merits? That was how everyone would see it and, in their position, so would she.

She had enough problems already; in banking women had built-in problems purely because of their sex. The men in banking had a whole string of prejudices against women being allowed to operate on their level; women didn't understand money, they didn't have the nerve to play the stock markets, they got married and left just when you had trained them, they didn't play golf. Often the reasons they gave for disliking to deal with women were very irrational, but those were often the deepest rooted; you could reason them out of their belief that women did not understand international finance, but you could not get at the deeply buried root of their prejudices, and that was where the crazy ideas were hidden.

'I think you're amazing,' said Baba. 'I don't understand banking at all; if Luke talks about what he's doing I don't understand a word—but he doesn't seem to mind that, he says he doesn't want to talk to me about money.' She giggled, and Judith eyed her with a wry smile.

'I'm sure he doesn't,' she said.

'I tried to show an interest, I thought he'd like to talk about his job, most men do, although they usually think women are too silly to understand business. But Luke's different.'

Judith smiled, thinking: oh, yes? That wasn't the impression she had got of him. Of course, she hadn't wanted to meet him anyway, but she was human; she resented the way he had run an eye over her, decided she didn't tempt him and then coolly proceeded to forget she existed. Not a typical male? Baba had to be fooling herself!

'I know most men think women are stupid, but Luke's personal assistant is a woman and he says he relies on her, trusts her completely. I was worried about her at first.' Baba wasn't amused any more, her blue eyes were wide and almost cold. 'She's very attractive and I could see she didn't like me, she gave me some very icy looks. I really tried to make friends with her, but she wasn't having it.'

'I shouldn't worry about her—he's marrying you. If he'd been at all interested in her he would have asked her, not you.' Judith tried to sound reassuring, but it sounded to her as though something had been going on between Luke Doulton and his assistant. It must have been a shock to all his lady friends when he asked Baba to marry him. He had been a bachelor for so long and then had got engaged to someone he had only just met. Judith couldn't help speculating about his emotional processes. She was surprised to find he had any emotions, beyond a dislike of people who tried to prise one of his possessions away from him.

'I suppose I'm worrying because it's the first time I've ever been in love,' Baba explained. 'Have you ever been in love, Judith?'

'Not that I've noticed,' said Judith, watching her flushed face with sympathy. Damn Luke Doulton if he didn't make her happy. Life is rarely as kind to anyone as it had been to Baba—she wasn't prepared for pain or unkindness, how would she react if she met it now?

CHAPTER TWO

DURING the next few days Judith was very busy; she found a flat only a quarter of an hour away from her grandmother's house and she bought a second-hand car which, the salesman assured her, without too much conviction, had been owned by an old lady who had rarely taken it out of the garage but had had it regularly serviced so that it was in perfect running order and had a very low mileage on the clock. Judith disregarded most of his assurances, but the car seemed to her to be a good buy at the price. She had not found it necessary to own a car while she lived in Manhattan; she took taxis if she wanted to get anywhere quickly and otherwise used public transport. At night it was too nerve-racking to use the subways, you never knew what you might run into, but if she went out with someone he usually ran her home afterwards anyway. Now that she was back in London she felt she would need a car; there was no direct bus route from her new flat to her grandmother's house.

The flat was in a large modern block; it was rather small but quite big enough for her and, as it had a tiny sitting-room, she would be able to entertain occasionally. She signed the lease and began to decorate it during the day; she had no intention of paying someone else to do what she could do herself. Her few odd bits of furniture, her ornaments and pictures and books, were still on their way across the Atlantic and heaven alone knew when they would finally show up, so she couldn't move in yet, but she wanted to stay with her grandmother as long as possible to help her get over the first shock of losing Granddad. She felt it would make life much easier if Mrs Murry had someone else around; just talking about her husband was something her grandmother seemed to need to do, and Judith was gradually hearing all about their lives together, things she had never heard before and which she found touching and moving and tinged with both sadness and joy. Mrs Murry's moods changed all the time; one minute she was smiling and telling funny stories about the past, the next she would get up and leave the room and Judith would be left guessing that upstairs, in her bedroom, her grandmother was crying. Those moments she never witnessed; Mrs Murry would not let you see her grief, you could only guess at it obliquely.

Judith persuaded her to come and choose wallpaper and paint; they discussed the colour scheme endlessly and Mrs Murry even came along to the flat once or twice and insisted on helping to scrape the old wallpaper off the walls. She did that with energy, perched on a chair; Judith watched her secretly to make sure she didn't tire herself out, but she knew better than to hint at such a thing. She got the feeling that her grandmother got a kick out of attacking the old wallpaper; Mrs Murry was releasing some of her rage against her husband's death, scowling as she scraped. Damn you, take that! her small face said as damp paper curled down and fell to the floor.

One day Judith had an interview with the managing director of the London office of her bank. He was brusque and slightly offhand; she sensed that he thought she was in a take-it-or-leave-it situation and had nowhere else to go and was therefore not intending to show any eagerness to have her working there again. Her place there was certainly open, but he made it clear that she would not be offered a salary anywhere near the one she had received in New York.

'American salaries are on a different scale,' he pointed out. 'I'm afraid we couldn't match what you've been getting.' He underlined how much he knew about her private position by asking: 'How is your grandmother? Beginning to get over her loss, I hope?' Although he smiled, Judith knew that he was pointing out that she needed a job if she was to stay in London to be near her grandmother, and she resented his attitude, without being surprised by it. She told him she would like a few days to consider the offer and left determined to see if she could get a job elsewhere. She was in an unusual position; she knew a great deal about the American stock market from having worked over there for several years, dealing with the New York end of it, and her expertise would give her an edge in London. She would have preferred to stay with the firm for which she had worked for so long, but not if it entailed taking a drop in salary and being treated the way she had been treated that morning. Judith was fascinated by the minutiae of banking and investments, she got a surge of adrenalin every time she took one of those calculated risks which are necessary if you are to make money, it was a form of gambling which could get into the blood if you weren't shrewd enough to add a cool-headed understanding of what you were doing to the flashes of guesswork which could make big money fast before the rest of the market has woken up to what is going on. It was only when you plunged heavily without having a background of solid information to back your hunch that you got into trouble. Judith *was* cool-headed, though; she studied world markets and world affairs all the time, she could look at a company balance sheet and see immediately whether they were under or over-valued and whether to buy or sell out.

'I'm good at my job, damn him, I don't like being treated as if I was a schoolgirl asking to be given a typist's job,' she told her own reflection that afternoon. She had just hung a new purchase in the flat. She had spotted it in a junk shop and bought it on impulse; an oval mirror framed in gilt acanthus leaves. It was early Victorian and solid, very heavy; she herself had carried it back to her flat and her arms had ached when she put it down, but she was delighted with it, partly because it had been a bargain. The man in the junk shop had cheerfully admitted he didn't like it, had too many old mirrors, they were a drug on the market and he was glad to get rid of it. 'I'm practically giving it to you,' he had said as Judith left, hugging it to her chest.

Tying her straight acorn brown hair back under a red cotton scarf, she made a face at herself in the mirror. 'I'll get a better job, don't worry,' she told her reflection, which didn't seem too convinced, her eyes distinctly looked worried.

She went off to paint woodwork; neatly dressed in jeans and an old shirt, her sleeves rolled up. She was so absorbed in what she was doing that when the doorbell rang she jumped, her paintbrush spattering white paint on her face. Impatiently rubbing the back of her hand across her cheek, she went to see who was at the door, and was amazed to see Baba.

'Oh, hallo! What are you doing here?' queried Judith before she realised that Baba had someone with her, a tall man at whom Judith glanced briefly before doing a double-take as she recognised him.

Baba giggled, 'You've got paint on your nose!'

Judith managed to smile, but it wasn't easy. Baba looked as ravishing and perfectly turned out as ever, she was wearing an immaculate white linen suit under which she wore nothing visible. The material lovingly hugged every curve of her body, and her thick blonde curls spilled down to her shoulders in a pretence of dishevelment which wouldn't fool anyone.

'We rang you at your grandmother's and she said you were here and told us the address.' Baba was looking past her at the open door of the sitting-room. 'Are you really redecorating the flat yourself? Aren't you clever? I wouldn't know where to start.' She sauntered past and Judith fell back, her paintbrush held out of danger in case it touched Baba's beautiful clothes. Luke Doulton closed the door. As his narrowed grey eyes assessed Judith's smouldering expression he looked amused.

The lazily mocking inspection put heated colour into her face. She marched after Baba, a sensation of instinctive fury filling her. This was turning out to be one of those days; what else could go wrong? At the back of her mind, she realised now, she had been debating whether or not to approach Luke Doulton's company for a job, but any idea of doing that had just been sunk without a trace. He would probably laugh like mad at the very idea, after seeing her looking such a sight.

'I'd offer you some coffee, but . . .' she began, and Baba, who had been looking around the room, turned with a smile, shaking her head.

'We can't stop, thanks, I just wanted to know whether you'd be at our party tonight or not. Your grandmother didn't seem to know anything about it and I . . .'

'Party? Tonight?' repeated Judith, and Baba stopped talking to stare at her.

'You did get my invitation? I wrote the card myself and it was posted with the others.'

'I didn't get an invitation,' Judith said flatly.

'You didn't? Oh, but . . . how irritating! It must have gone astray in the post, maybe I didn't have the right address. The party's tonight. Can you make it?' Baba looked at her pleadingly, biting her lower lip. 'Oh, do try to be there—most of the guests are Luke's friends and I want some of mine to come too. Ruth will be much happier if you're there, she's a bit nervous, she's never been to the Savoy before.'

Aware of Luke Doulton prowling around the room behind her, staring at the wallpaper and the half completed paintwork, Judith couldn't think clearly. 'Well, I'd love to, of course . . .'

Before she could add the 'but' which was hovering on her lips Baba burst in eagerly, 'Oh, that's terrific! It should be a great evening, shouldn't it, Luke?'

'It certainly won't be dull,' he said in a deep voice. Judith heard the New England accent with something of a shock, which was absurd, because she knew very well that he was an American, but she had already got used to hearing English voices all around her again and to hear that familiar accent took her by surprise.

As she looked round at him he moved into a patch of sunlight which showed her his thick hair, a rich dark brown with an almost reddish tinge and threads of silver which gleamed as the sunlight streamed through the windows behind him. Judith felt dwarfed, he towered over her. He must be well over six foot tall, she thought, and every inch of him seemed to be bone and muscle. He was wearing a well-cut lounge suit, a dark grey with a hint of a paler stripe in it, but beneath the immaculate formality of the clothes his shoulders were wide and powerful, his body leanly fit. He was a very impressive male animal, Baba might almost have been designed to hang on his arm. She was nestling close to him at that second, her hand slipping up his sleeve in a confidently possessive gesture, very female beside that aggressive masculinity.

'Judith has just got back from New York—I told you, didn't I, darling? She's in banking, she's terribly clever, she knows all about investments and that sort of thing.'

Judith's teeth met, and she forced a polite smile as Luke Doulton stared at her, his brows lifting.

'I gather you were with Schewitz and Quayle?'

She nodded.

'Handling clients?'

Judith nodded again.

'Are you transferring to their London office?'

'Possibly; I'm thinking about it.' She felt distinctly at a disadvantage in her paint-stained jeans, with a gaudy scarf tied round her head and white paint on her nose. Quite apart from the obvious fact that she was no beauty, her appearance would hardly inspire confidence in her ability. She looked a mess, and she felt so furious she could have broken things. Baba shouldn't have sprung Luke Doulton on her. If she had known she was going to run into him she would have spent hours getting ready; he wasn't going to get the chance to call her 'office furniture' again.

'Feel like a change, do you?' he asked in a slow drawl, and she watched the way his mouth curled up at the sides. His cheekbones were hard, angular beneath his tanned skin; his firm, well-shaped mouth conveyed a cynical amusement. The last time she had seen him, at the 21 Club, he had radiated threat, those eyes dangerous as he talked to poor John. Now he was relaxed, exuding charm, but only a fool would forget that Luke Doulton could be dangerous and Judith hoped she was no fool.

'Couldn't you find her a job, darling?' Baba coaxed, leaning against him like a small, confiding cat, and he looked down at her with aware, amused sensuality. Judith got the impression he enjoyed looking at Baba, but she still did not get the feeling he was as madly in love with her as his sudden proposal suggested.

'I won't have any trouble finding a job,' Judith said tightly. 'Thanks all the same.' She moved towards the door pointedly. 'Thanks for the invitation—I'll see you at the party, Baba.'

They followed her; the sound of their footsteps very loud in the flat, which echoed with every tiny noise in the way that rooms do when they hold no furniture. Luke's head only just cleared the sill of the door, Judith noted, and although he was still smiling she found it nerve-racking to have him around.

He halted and looked down at her, one brow curving quizzically. 'Why don't we have lunch and talk about your career? I'm free this Friday. How about you?'

Judith was taken aback, she hadn't expected him to take Baba's coaxing seriously, and she didn't know if she wanted to have lunch alone with him, anyway. He bothered her.

'Thank you, but . . .'

'Monday any better?' he broke in before she had finished the sentence, and Judith hesitated, meeting those cool grey eyes and realising suddenly that Baba hadn't pushed him into this. Luke Doulton wasn't the type of guy who could be pushed into anything, he was serious about interviewing her for his own reasons, which had nothing whatever to do with Baba.

'Yes, that would be fine,' she said slowly, thinking hard. She wasn't sure she was going to be very happy about his motives for being interested in her, but at least it would not be humiliating to accept the lunch invitation now that she knew he was offering it for his own reasons and not because Baba was twisting his arm. It couldn't do any harm to find out what was behind his interest; having lunch didn't commit her to anything.

'Eight o'clock tonight at the Savoy, remember.' said Baba, smiling delightedly. From her expression it was clear that she was under the illusion that she was totally reponsible for the lunch invitation. Judith smiled back, allowing her to go on thinking so.

'Thanks, Baba.' She might have been livid about Baba's blatant manoeuvring, but she knew Baba meant well; and anyway it was quite impossible to go on being angry with Baba about anything, especially when she glowed with such obvious delight in her own cleverness.

'I'll see you tonight,' said Baba as she and Luke walked away, but just as Judith was closing the front door she hurried back to whisper softly: 'Don't mention the film to Luke, promise?'

Judith looked at her in surprise. She had forgotten all about the possibility that Baba would be making a film. 'Okay,' she said, wondering why Baba was keeping it a secret from her fiancé.

'I forgot—you haven't seen the ring,' said Baba far more loudly and obviously intending Luke to hear that part of their conversation. 'What do you think?' She held out her hand and Judith gasped at the size and beauty of the emerald, a square-cut stone surrounded by small diamonds, in a delicate gold setting.

'Fantastic—it's beautiful!'

Baba whispered: 'I'm keeping the film a secret until it's certain, you see.' She looked into Judith's eyes appealingly. 'Thank you,' she said in that louder voice, 'See you tonight, then!'

Going back to her painting, Judith managed to stop herself from dwelling on Luke Doulton's invitation; she had the sort of mind which can keep a tight rein over its own activities, which possibly explained why she had been so successful in banking. Her only real drawbacks, as far as her career went, were her sense of humour and her independence, neither of which met with much appreciation from the men she worked with. Judith had learnt to hide her rebellious streak behind a bland exterior. Any mockery she felt was concealed in public;

business men were often the very last people able to laugh at themselves and they hated to feel they were being laughed at, particularly by a woman.

That evening she flicked wryly through her wardrobe, looking for something suitable to wear at the party. She chose a dark red dress with a Victorian, demurely romantic style; full sleeves ending in a layered frill at the wrist and a low neckline partly filled with foamy white lace, the skirts full and flounced. It was a dress she had bought in New York at a small boutique on Fifth Avenue; the next time she went back there the shop had vanished and there was a druggist there—but that was New York for you, she hadn't been surprised.

She had a leisurely bath and was getting dressed when the phone went. 'It's Ruth,' Mrs Murry called up the stairs a few moments later. 'She says do you want a lift?'

'I'd love one,' said Judith. 'Then I can get drunk if I like . . .'

'I hope you're joking,' Mrs Murry said with disapproval before vanishing to relay her reply to Ruth.

Judith spent some time doing her face and hair; no amount of effort was going to make her look like Baba, but she wasn't displeased with the end result in the mirror. Her hair fell, sleek and smooth, to her shoulders, curling inwards slightly against her cheek. Her dark eyes had more lustre than usual with a warm brown shadow on the lids, and she had carefully given her face more colour, blusher on her cheekbones and a glossy red brushed on to her lips.

She was relieved to be going with Ruth and David; it would have been ghastly going in to the party on her own. As she heard the doorbell downstairs she gave herself another last long stare, then moved to leave the room, her skirts rustling. Ruth was talking to Mrs Murry in the hall, and they both turned to look up at Judith as she joined them.

'You look wonderful,' Ruth said quickly; too quickly, Judith thought, as she returned the smile. Ruth was very kind, but Judith's more realistic appraisal of herself was not altered by the compliment. When she was in her teens she had often looked into mirrors with despair, wishing there was some magic which would change her from a gangling, skinny adolescent into a beautiful woman. She had grown up knowing she would never be beautiful; with time and effort she could look interesting, even quite attractive, and that was all. Whenever someone paid her a compliment she put it under the microscope of her own intelligence and then dismissed it; she might never be beautiful, but she did not intend to be stupid, or to let anyone make a fool of her.

'Lucky for Baba that you're safely married, or Luke Doulton might fall for you,' she told Ruth teasingly, and Ruth laughed, looking down at her pretty yellow dress with open satisfaction. She still had that cuddly, warmhearted appeal which had made boys flock around her before she married; the yellow dress suited her perfectly.

When they got into the car David turned in the driving seat and grinned at Judith. 'Will you look at me? You've made me dress up as a penguin, why is it that women can't enjoy themselves unless they've made men thoroughly uncomfortable?'

'You look very handsome,' Judith assured him.

'May God forgive you!'

'You do! All the girls are going to fall in love with you on first sight.'

'Watch your tongue,' Ruth told her, and David laughed, switching on the engine.

'Now she's worried. I may have a fantastic evening, if I can compete with the wonderful Luke Doulton, that is—some chance! I don't happen to have a billion pounds in my bank balance. Isn't it amazing what an aphrodisiac money is?'

'Don't be so cynical. He's a very good-looking guy too,' Ruth said.

David made a noise and Ruth poked him, leaning forward. 'He is, you can't deny it—isn't he, Judith?'

'He's not bad,' Judith admitted reluctantly, and got a very reproachful look from Ruth.

'How can you be so half-hearted? Baba said all the other models are jealous of her, and not because of his money. They fancy him, she said.'

'Come on, darling, if he was four foot three and as bald as an egg he would still have women chasing him for his money. I'll admit he's a pleasant enough man, he was very friendly when he came to see us. I've got nothing personal against him, but don't expect me to rave about him, because I refuse.' David sounded irritable, and Judith wondered if he was sick of having his wife talk about Luke. No doubt little else had engaged her attention since Baba told her she was engaged to him. David had always been a quiet, faintly wry man who tended to watch what went on rather than join in; he was rather attractive himself, so he had no real reason for being jealous of Luke Doulton. In his evening suit he was very distinguished; he had a slim, lithe figure.

'I hate big parties,' he said defensively as his car headed for the Strand. It was thick with traffic at this hour of the evening; many people were still making their way to theatres. Judith looked down the wide road and saw the neon flash of theatre signs and fast food take-aways, the nose-to-tail cars slowly inching their way towards Aldwych. 'I'll try and park down on the Embankment,' David thought aloud. 'Shall I drop you two at the Savoy and then go off and find a parking space? I can join you later.'

'That would be best; I wouldn't be able to walk far in these shoes,' Ruth admitted. She was wearing delicate silver sandals with perilously high heels.

David turned into the Savoy forecourt; above them Judith saw the elegant silver facade of the hotel, like a giant Rolls-Royce. The commissionaire opened the door and she and Ruth slid out, a slight wind catching Judith's dress and ruffling it.

'See you as soon as I can park,' said David before he backed and rejoined the stream of traffic passing outside.

As the two women went into the hotel Ruth whispered: 'I'm so nervous! Are you? You don't look it, but then I suppose in New York you got used to places like this . . .'

Judith glanced around and one of the hotel staff came over with a smile. 'May I help you, madam?'

'Yes, we're guests at Mr Doulton's party,' Judith told him, and his smile widened.

'Of course, madam, Mr Doulton is using one of our private suites—I'll send a pageboy to show you the way.' He glanced at their fur jackets. 'The cloakroom is down here, madam, if you would care to leave your coats.'

Judith stood, glancing around her, while Ruth was in the ladies' room powdering her nose. The hotel had a distinctive period feel; you half expected Noël Coward to come sauntering out of the lifts at any moment. The décor and ambiance was strictly of the nineteen-twenties.

They heard the party before they arrived; the room was already crowded with people and Judith's first glance around the faces told her that she knew a number of them by sight. They were mostly very rich people whose faces appeared in newspapers; financiers, film stars, jet-setters. Well, had she expected Luke

Doulton to invite nobodies to his party? she asked herself with a cynical twist of her lips.

'Hallo,' said Luke, catching the smile before she could shut it off. 'I hope you're going to enjoy yourself.' His grey eyes mocked her and the ambiguous ring of the question made it clear he doubted that very much.

'Oh, I'm sure I'll find plenty to amuse me,' Judith said sweetly, and watched his firm mouth curl in amused enjoyment.

'Let me introduce you to some of my friends,' he offered, glancing around.

'Oh, please don't,' she refused. 'I'll just prowl around and see what I come up with, thanks.'

Baba was talking to Ruth a few feet away. She turned and gave Judith a neon smile, her eyes so bright she looked as if she might burn out at any minute. Judith wondered how she managed to move in the skin-tight wild silk dress; her tanned arms and face looked superb against the white silk, but Judith would never have dared to buy a dress that tight. You needed a figure like Baba to show it off, but how on earth did she walk? Slowly, it appeared, as Baba joined them, one step at a time, her body swaying.

'You look terrific,' Judith told her, and Baba laughed, delighted.

'Thanks, so do you—doesn't she, Luke?'

Judith met his gaze wryly. He ran his eyes deliberately from head to foot and Judith did a slow burn at the cool inspection, when his gaze came back to her face she was icy with resentment. 'Yes,' he said. 'On second thoughts maybe I'd better not introduce you to any of my friends, they're mostly with their wives. I wouldn't want to ruin some happy marriages.'

Baba laughed, but Judith was not amused, he didn't mean a word of that, but she wouldn't let him make fun of her and get away with it.

'I'm not the home-wrecker type,' she said, looking around the room and thinking that there wasn't one man there who looked interesting, anyway. Her eyes picked out one man under forty, though, whose face looked vaguely familiar although she couldn't put a name to it. She stared and felt him become aware of her, his hazel eyes focusing on her. Judith turned back to Ruth.

'Let's circulate, shall we? See you later, Baba.' She moved away and Ruth fell into step. A waiter offered them a tray of champagne; they each took one and as they sipped the golden wine someone halted beside them.

'Hallo, we've met, haven't we?' It was the man she had spotted a moment ago and she wasn't really surprised at his appearance. She smiled at him, her head to one side.

'I thought I'd seen you before.' He was a slim, broad-shouldered man in his thirties with fair hair and a good-tempered smile, his hazel eyes lively and warm. He wasn't handsome, but he had a face Judith liked immediately.

'I'm Robert Gordon—you're with Schewitz and Quayle, aren't you? I'm afraid I don't remember your name.'

'Judith Murry.' He was offering his hand, she shook it, then introduced Ruth. 'When did we meet?' Judith asked him after he had shaken hands and smiled at Ruth.

'John Atkins acted for us when my company went public four years ago. I met you several times in meetings with John to discuss the launch.'

It was the sort of negotiation which the bank handled frequently; Judith couldn't remember him—but then the occasion would have been much more important to him, he probably remembered it vividly whereas to her it had just been another business deal.

'Do you know everyone here, Mr Gordon?' Judith asked him.

'Robert,' he insisted, smiling at her. 'No, I hardly know a soul; I was so relieved to see you, at least I knew who you were and had some excuse for coming over.'

She laughed. 'I know how you feel—we were just wondering how we were going to get through the evening.'

'You should have brought your boy-friend,' he said, glancing at her ringless hand.

Their eyes met and Judith gave him a dry smile; he was fishing, but she had no intention of letting him catch anything.

'You're here alone, too,' Ruth said alertly. 'No wife, Robert?'

Judith could have kicked her. He smiled, shaking his head. Ruth's smile widened as she looked back at Judith, her eyes saying: there! He's free and you can have him if you want him. Judith stared back without a blink, pretending not to get the message which Ruth was sending so insistently. Ruth seemed to think she must be desperate; it was time Judith disillusioned her. Looking away, Ruth spotted David making his way through the throng and her face lit up.

'Oh, there's my husband—excuse me, won't you?'

Judith looked after her as she darted away, her spine tingling with irritation. Ruth was being ludicrously obvious, deliberately leaving her alone with Robert.

'How's John Atkins? I heard he went to the States,' Robert remarked, and Judith looked back at him, nodding.

'We both did—I've just come back, but John's staying there; he's doing very well in New York.'

'Why did you come back? A better job?'

'My grandfather died; family obligations, you know . . .'

'Where are you working now?' Robert asked when she had finished explaining why she had returned to England, and she shrugged.

'I'm taking a brief sabbatical before I take up one of the offers I've had.' It sounded much better than telling him frankly that she didn't like the only solid offer she had had.

'If you're still taking offers you might come in and talk to me one day—we would be very interested in having someone with your qualifications; you must be quite an expert on the American market by now.' Robert fished into his inside pocket and produced a flat card case, extracting a card he handed it to her. 'Give me a ring and let me give you lunch; even if you don't want to join us I'd like to have a chance to talk to you somewhere quieter than this.' He looked around the noisy room with a grimace.

Judith studied the card, her curiosity aroused as she saw the name of his firm. She remembered him now; she vividly recalled the occasion when the firm went public, they had been so successful that they had needed capital badly to be able to expand and, judging by their quoted price on the market at the moment, their success had continued.

'Thank you,' she said slowly.

Robert watched her face. 'I'm serious,' he stressed. 'Tell you what—give me your phone number and I'll ring you, otherwise you might forget.'

She laughed. 'I won't forget.'

'Promise?' He had moved closer and was looking down at her with what was more than a business interest; his hazel eyes held a very attractive smile. His face was deceptively formed, the muscle and bone beneath his skin gave his features a solid look which the humour and warmth of his eyes denied. He wore his fair hair cut very short, but it had a tendency to curl tightly against his scalp, although she could see that he had brushed it down flat with great vigour. Judith liked what she saw, she smiled back at him and nodded.

'Promise.'

He stayed with her when Ruth and David joined them ten minutes later. Ruth had obviously decided she had left them alone long enough; her matchmaking, although blatant, was not selfless, she was bored with watching from a distance and wanted to check and see how they were doing. Judith got the distinct impression that Robert knew exactly what was in Ruth's mind; as Ruth looked eagerly from one to the other of them he glanced at Judith with a glint in his hazel eyes. Judith grinned at him; by now she knew enough about him to be sure he would grin back, and he did. Ruth looked very satisfied, she didn't know why they were grinning at each other like that, but she could see that they were sharing private jokes, and that was just great, her little conspiracy had worked. She couldn't believe that Judith was happy working with such dull things as share prices and market quotations; Ruth wanted to see her safely married, it would give them something in common again. Ruth was so contented that she could not imagine any other way of being happy than to be married with two children; and sometimes Judith wondered if she could be right. But she could see no point in getting married for its own sake; you had to be sure the man was someone you would never get bored with or stop loving, and that was a feeling Judith had never had for anyone she had dated.

Looking across the room towards Baba, she hoped Baba had made the right choice; that she hadn't been dazzled by Luke Doulton's worldly possessions; by his money, his power, his glamour, because if she had Baba

was going to be unhappy when she woke up and
realised that all those things did not make a safe basis
for a good relationship. Once she got used to Luke's
way of life she would start to see him as he was behind
all the glitter. Maybe he would be as charming and
attractive as he seemed, but maybe he was nothing of
the kind. He had to be a very tough man to have
survived in the jungle he inhabited, and would a man
like that make Baba happy? Judith frowned, studying
them both. Perhaps he would; perhaps Baba was
precisely the sort of woman he needed and had been
looking for. After all, she was sweet-tempered and
placid. Luke could be sure he wouldn't get any hassle
from her, she wouldn't make waves, she was obviously
easy to live with and he must get all the trouble he
needed when he was at work. Maybe what he saw in
Baba was the promise of a peaceful home life, not to
mention a beauty that made heads turn everywhere she
went. Baba's combination of beauty and good temper
was a rare one, and Luke Doulton would want an
exceptional woman.

While Judith was watching them Luke had been
talking to a new arrival; a tall, elegant woman in her
late twenties with sleek black hair swept up behind her
head and pinned there with a pearl clasp. Her black
dress had chic, it went with the slightly arrogant cast of
her features: the high cheekbones, perfectly modelled
nose and rather cold mouth. Judith wondered what was
being said; Baba was looking uneasy and although
Judith couldn't see Luke's face she saw his long body
stiffen with tension and the muscles in the back of his
neck were rigid.

'I wonder who that is,' said Ruth with the uneasiness
which you could see in Baba's expression.

'That's his assistant, Caroline Rendell,' Robert told
them drily.

Judith looked at him sharply and he made a wry face. 'Luke always picks girls who look a million dollars,' he said, then gave Ruth a hurried smile, remembering that she was Baba's sister. 'These days the office staff have to impress the clients,' he joked, but Ruth didn't look much happier.

'Baba *said* she was good-looking,' she said, half to herself.

Judith watched Caroline Rendell's icy face; it wore a little smile, but there was nothing humorous or pleasant in the movement of her lips. Judith felt sure she was saying something very acid, the girl looked as if acid remarks came easily to her.

'I don't like the look of her,' Ruth commented.

'Join the club.' Judith glanced at Robert. 'Have you met her?'

'I met her—she didn't appear to be meeting me. Every time I've seen her since she's ignored me. I don't think I measure up to her standards; to get noticed by Miss Rendell you have to be a multi-millionaire!'

Judith laughed. 'I believe you.' That was the impression she had got, too. Caroline Rendell looked ambitious and cold; she also looked as if she was bitterly angry with Luke Doulton and she was making no pretence about it which, if she was a really clever woman, she would have done, because although Judith barely knew him, it seemed clear that Luke Doulton was not a man who would look kindly on anyone who embarrassed or annoyed him.

She glanced back at the little group and saw that Caroline Rendell had walked away and Luke was facing her now. His face was blank, but Judith watched those grey eyes of his and she almost felt sorry for Caroline Rendell; that was the look Judith had first seen when her bank was engaged in attempting to put together a take-over bid for one of Luke Doulton's companies. He was hiding his rage better at the moment, forcing it out of sight by an effort of will, but Judith felt it coming across the room in waves. Caroline Rendell had made a bad mistake. Whatever had been going on between her and Luke Doulton he hadn't chosen to marry her; making some sort of public scene, however discreetly, had been stupid. It wouldn't alter his decision, it would merely make him angry; Caroline must have been beside herself with temper not to understand that.

Suddenly Luke's grey eyes actually focused on Judith; she felt a leap of attention inside him, he was looking at her, his eyes narrowing, and for a brief second she stared back, wondering why he was looking at her like that, then she looked away because, even at this distance, Luke Doulton was overpowering, she felt the room shrink so that she almost seemed to be standing next to him.

Not long afterwards he and Baba came over to join them, bringing a small group of people in their wake. Judith and Robert politely stepped back while Luke introduced his sisters and their husbands to Ruth and David. Everyone kept smiling, but the talk was stilted. Luke's sisters were younger than their brother. The eldest, Pauline, was in her early thirties but looked younger, her smooth hair a definite red, her skin a heavy white and her green eyes slanting under fine dark brows.

'Gracious, what a daring little dress,' she said to Baba. 'How do you manage to walk in it?' Judith suppressed a smile; it was her own question, but she had not cared to deliver it so bluntly.

'It's a fabulous dress,' the other sister said quickly before Baba could answer. 'Who made it for you?' Judith had already decided she preferred the younger sister; Angela was more like Luke in her colouring, her hair the same dark brown and her eyes wide and grey. She was pregnant, she had told Baba a moment ago, wasn't it sickening to have to wear tents for months on end? Baba had asked: 'It's your second baby, isn't it?' and Angela had said ruefully: 'Third, darling, third.' Pauline, it seemed, had one son aged twelve who was away at boarding school, and she told Angela that one was enough. 'Three is ridiculous!' Angela made a wicked face at her, eyes defiant, and Judith laughed, which was a mistake because Luke glanced at her across the circle and decided to introduce her.

'An investments expert?' queried Pauline, brows rising. 'Really? I didn't know women did jobs like that. You must be horribly clever.' She made it sound like an accusation. Judith felt Luke watching her, waiting to see how she would reply.

'Oh, I am,' she said with bland indifference to Pauline's opinion, and Luke laughed softly. 'We're not *all* pinbrains, you know,' Judith added, and Pauline stared at her in apparent stupefaction while she worked that out. Well, at least, thought Judith, she was getting *some* fun out of the evening.

CHAPTER THREE

The following Monday Judith had lunch with Luke Doulton at a small and very fashionable restaurant in Mayfair. She had come armoured, with a very shrewd idea of why he wanted to talk to her. After the occasion when Schewitz and Quayle put together the take-over bid for his company Luke had a grudge against the bank; Judith would be very surprised if his interest in her did not have something to do with a long-term hostility for her old firm. She was going to listen to him, mainly out of curiosity, but she had no intention of allowing him to use her in whatever conspiracy he was planning. Her years with the bank had left her with a good deal of private information about their dealings, their clients, their staff. If Luke Doulton was planning something connected with Schewitz and Quayle he would no doubt find her a very useful tool; but Judith's hackles rose at the thought of being used for any such purpose. She had a strong loyalty towards the New York house; she might be irritated with the managing director in London, but her annoyance did not extend to a backstairs intrigue with Luke Doulton.

He was sitting in the small, circular bar attached to the restaurant and rose as she appeared. She shook hands, noting the firm warm clasp. He had good hands; strong and long-fingered, the backs of them lightly dusted with dark hairs. Today he was wearing one of those formal grey lounge suits and a blue-striped shirt with a pale grey silk tie; he looked elegant and businesslike.

'What can I get you to drink?' he asked as she sat down and the waiter appeared with two menus.

Judith took one of the menus and thought briefly; better not to drink too much, she might need all her wits about her.

'I'll have a Lillet,' she said, and the waiter bowed and vanished to get her a glass of the lightly flavoured wine.

'I hope you weren't too bored at the party; I saw that you'd met a friend. How did you meet Robert Gordon? Through the bank? One of their clients, is he?'

'Yes,' said Judith, opening the menu. 'Gracious, how does one find one's way through a list this long? Is the food as good as it sounds?'

She felt his quick glance, the narrowed eyes with which he registered her evasion of his question, but he accepted the change of subject without comment and they read the menu while they sipped their drinks and talked very little. Judith had already seen Robert again; he had rung her on the Saturday morning after the party and asked her out to dinner. 'Not business,' he had said, and laughed. It had been a very enjoyable evening, they had mainly talked about the States, swapping stories about hotels they knew and cities they had either loved or hated. Robert travelled a great deal; he was an entertaining companion.

When she and Luke had ordered they finished their drinks and went through into the restaurant. Judith was aware of heads turning, eyes following them. Luke was well known and his engagement party had made the gossip columns the day afterwards; in print it had sounded far more glamorous and exciting than it had been in actual fact. Reading about it, Judith had wondered if she had gone to a different party. The gossip columnists had apparently seen a lot she missed.

She knew she wasn't going to be mistaken for one of his girl-friends; she was dressed today in a very businesslike russet wool dress. Nobody was going to have dark suspicions about Luke's interest in *her*; the last thing she wanted was to try to compete with girls like Baba or Caroline Rendell.

Over their first course Luke told her: 'I've just lost my personal assistant.' His tone was dispassionate and calm; if Judith hadn't witnessed the little scene at the party she would never have guessed that anything lay behind his sudden announcement.

So much for Caroline Rendell, she thought, her mouth indenting and her dark eyes lowered to hide their amusement. Before you throw stones you should make sure you don't live in a glasshouse. Luke hadn't lost any time in despatching Caroline; when he used a knife he did so with ruthless speed and efficiency, no doubt.

'Did I say something funny?' he asked, taking her by surprise.

She looked up, eyes startled, then recovered and said blandly: 'I'm sure you would never do that.'

He regarded her for a moment in silence. 'You have a very interesting mind,' he said, surprising her again.

'Thank you,' she said demurely.

'Do you want the job?' The question was a frontal assault; although she had guessed it might be coming she hadn't expected it so fast and with so little preliminaries or window-dressing.

Her eyes widened further, she quickly looked down. 'What exactly would it entail?'

'A salary twice whatever you've been getting,' he said drily.

When he offered temptation he certainly did it in style, Judith decided. Aloud she asked: 'Shall we discuss the job before we talk about money?'

'You've got all the qualifications I need; you have a brain or you wouldn't have been doing the work you have been doing. You're obviously capable of working on your own, which is what you might well be doing a good deal when I'm away from my desk. I'd want you based in London, I have to fly around the world most of the time and I'd rely on you to keep me posted with what was happening over here while I was gone. The work would be far more varied than you have been doing; although you would be working with investments part of the time there's a great deal more to it than that. You'd be expected to make confidential reports on companies I'm interested in; I'd want those daily, wherever I was. To put it briefly, you'd be my eyes and ears in London and, to some extent, my brains as well.'

He hadn't so much as mentioned Schewitz and Quayle; she wondered whether to bring them up and see his reaction, but decided to wait a while and listen to whatever else he had to say. She went on with her strips of beef cooked in wine and cream while he talked and, somehow, managed to eat his filet mignon at the same time. Judith asked questions and got concise and clear answers, but the subject of her old firm never came up. Had she imagined his hostility to them? she wondered. Or was he being very oblique and cunning by hiding what he really wanted from her?

'You can have three days to decide,' he told her as they drank their coffee. 'Then I shall have to look for someone else; it's a matter of some urgency as my previous assistant has already left.'

Judith gave him a dry smile. 'I see.' Had Caroline resigned or was she thrown out? she wondered. The woman must be crazy to let her personal emotions ruin her career, but maybe she had got a job just as good with someone else, her experience with Luke Doulton would no doubt have made her an attractive prospect for one of his rivals.

'Ring me on Thursday morning,' he said, and she nodded. He glanced at his watch. 'I'll have to be shooting off soon; I have an appointment at three-thirty. We have time for some more coffee, though.' He turned to signal the waiter and Judith saw his eyes flash after a girl who was walking through the crowded restaurant. She was a very pretty girl, her figure swayed enticingly as she moved, and Luke Doulton observed it with interest. Judith frowned; poor Baba, she got the feeling Luke was not the faithful kind.

The waiter hurried over and Luke turned back to face Judith, catching her with her brows together in that frown.

'Something wrong?' he asked, staring.

She didn't have to answer; the waiter leaned over to refill her cup with strong black coffee, and by the time he had departed Luke had forgotten his question. A few minutes later he signed the bill and they left.

'My car's outside, can I give you a lift?' he asked. 'If you don't mind coming along to my office my driver will take you on wherever you want to go.'

She got into the long, silvery limousine and watched Luke light a thin cigar, the pale wreaths of blue smoke fragrant as they drifted to her nostrils. 'You should wear red more often, it suits you,' he said suddenly, and she looked at him with widening eyes, startled by the personal remark. 'I liked the dress you wore at the party; that's the sort of dress that suits you.' He held the cigar between finger and thumb, rolling it slightly, while he studied her coolly. 'You're much too thin; do you diet? You don't need to, you know.'

'Thanks for the advice,' said Judith, eyeing him with dislike. She saw his mouth curl up and his grey eyes slid sideways to mock her.

'If you're going to work for me I feel I have some right to an opinion on your appearance.'

'Oh, do you?' she said, making it clear she did not agree. 'I haven't made up my mind yet. I have other offers to consider.'

'You'll accept mine,' he said with what she felt was staggering complacency.

'Oh, will I?'

'Yes.'

'What makes you so sure?'

'I want you, and I always get what I want,' he said, and the limousine halted smoothly outside a block of skyscraper offices. Luke Doulton smiled at Judith and said: 'I'll hear from you by Thursday,' then he had opened the door and was gone. The car drove on a moment later and took Judith back to her new flat. When she was alone she sat on a packing case and stared around her. Some of her possessions had arrived from America, she hadn't unpacked them yet because the flat was not ready for occupation, although she didn't imagine it would take her long to finish the redecorating. She approved her new wallpaper absently while her mind was sorting through what Luke Doulton had said to her.

She was tempted; she had to admit that. The salary was one of the major attractions, but the job itself sounded fascinating. It would involve heavy responsibilities, but then that didn't worry Judith, she enjoyed work which offered her the chance to work on her own and take responsibility. There were two real drawbacks; one of them was Luke himself. Judith didn't want to like him, but she did, and that was dangerous, because he belonged to Baba and Judith didn't steal other women's men. That was a minor matter, though. The real problem was that she wasn't sure that he did not plan to use her, somehow, against her old firm. If she could be certain that that was not in her mind she would jump at the job. Her feeling of attraction to Luke really didn't matter; even if she hadn't been the sort of girl who doesn't poach she knew Luke Doulton wouldn't be interested in her.

She wasn't in his league. A woman had to be very beautiful to catch his eye.

There was a great deal about him she did not like, however. She hadn't liked the way he said: 'I want you and I always get what I want.' That had been a revelation of how his mind worked that had struck her forcibly; it hadn't surprised her, because his assurance and arrogance were visible in spite of his charm and the humour she saw in his eyes at times. For half an hour she sat on the packing case and added up Luke Doulton like a company balance sheet: he was cynical and ruthless and without hesitation in going after what he wanted, whether it was a woman like Baba or a company which he felt would make him even more money. Judith liked his directness in some ways, she liked the occasional surprise he had given her when they talked; he had treated her with more respect than she sometimes met with from the men in her world. He didn't imply that she had a drawback because she was a woman; he had taken her on her own terms, and that was very much a plus factor. She looked hard for the flaws in him, she would only take this job with her eyes wide open. But by the time she went back to have the evening meal with her grandmother she knew she wanted that job.

She had lunch with Robert next day. They discussed the job he was offering her and Judith half hoped he would suggest a salary which would make his job more attractive than the one Luke offered, but he didn't, of course, and with reluctance she had to turn him down.

'You're going back to Schewitz and Quayle, then, I suppose?' he said with flattering regret before they parted.

'I doubt it,' said Judith, not yet willing to tell him about Luke's job.

'Playing your cards close to your chest?' he suggested,

smiling. 'Well, whatever you decide to do I hope you'll let me take you to the theatre next week? Are you free on Tuesday?'

Judith was and accepted. She liked Robert and wanted to see him again.

On the Wednesday evening she was listening to a record when the phone went. She answered it; her grandmother had already gone up to bed because she had a headache.

'Judith?' Baba sounded distraught, and Judith frowned.

'Hallo, Baba, something wrong?'

'I have to talk to you—can I come round to see you now?'

'I suppose so.' Judith looked at her watch, it was after nine. 'How long will it take you to get here?'

'Half an hour. It isn't inconvenient, is it? I'm sorry to be a nuisance, but . . .'

'That's okay, come over.' Judith replaced the phone, her eyes thoughtful. She finished listening to the record and then went into the kitchen and made some coffee. Baba must have a pressing reason for wanting to talk to her; what had gone wrong? Why did she want to confide in Judith, rather than Ruth?

The door bell went and Judith opened the door to find Baba, wrapped in a short blue suede jacket, looking agitated. 'Oh, Judith, I'm so sorry to barge in on you at this time of night . . .'

'Don't be silly, come in and have some coffee—I've just made it.'

Baba followed her into the kitchen and perched on a stool, her shapely legs curled round the metal legs of the stool. Judith poured her some coffee and pushed it over to her. 'Why don't we go into the sitting-room? It would be more comfortable.'

'I won't stop long, it's just that I have to talk to you.'

Baba followed her out of the kitchen, her cup in her hand, and a visible urgency in her face. 'You remember that film I told you about? They want me to do a screen test, they rang tonight and asked me to fly over to California tomorrow and I don't know what to do.'

'Aren't you able to go? A job lined up?'

'It isn't that—it's Luke. He won't be pleased when he hears. He wants me to stop work once we're married, you see; he won't want me to take the part in this film.'

'I wouldn't have thought he was so old-fashioned,' said Judith, rather surprised. 'He didn't give me the impression that he disapproved of women working.' On the contrary, she had been favourably struck by his lack of bias where working women were concerned. Did he have two standards—one for most women and the other for his own wife?

'Oh, I don't think he does in general, but you see he wants to start a family right away.' Baba looked at her and laughed, going pink. 'He's keen to have children, he doesn't want to wait a few years. He asked me if I'd mind having a baby right away.'

Judith's eyes opened wide. 'How forthright of him. What did you say?'

'I thought it was rather sweet. I said I didn't mind, I'd like a baby too. I didn't know about the film possibility then. I'm getting a bit bored with modelling; it can be very tiring and I've done all that. I rather liked the idea of having a baby, but now . . .'

'Now you think you'd rather make a film,' said Judith with amusement, and Baba looked at her blankly without humour.

'Yes, that's the problem. I daren't tell Luke about the screen test, but I can't pass up this opportunity, it could lead to anything. I don't know what to do.'

'Tell him and go off and have your test—that's what you want to do, so why not do it?'

'It's so easy for you,' Baba sighed. 'Your career matters more to you than anything else anyway; I don't see you hesitating between your job and a man.'

Judith's brows rose, but she didn't dispute the assumption, although she resented it.

Baba looked at her uncertainly. 'Luke told me he'd offered you Caroline's job; are you going to accept?'

'I haven't made up my mind.' Judith knew she wasn't quite telling the truth; she had made up her mind, but she wasn't going to commit herself just yet.

'Oh, do, Judith—then I could go away for a few weeks without worrying; I'm scared of her—you should have heard what she said to me at our engagement party!' Baba's voice was shaking slightly, she bit her lip. 'She said . . .'

'I can imagine,' Judith said quickly when Baba paused, her voice too unsteady for her to go on. 'Don't worry about her, that's stupid. Remember, she's a woman scorned, whatever she said was meant to hurt you and if you let it get to you then she will have succeeded.'

'They had an affair,' Baba said flatly. 'Luke didn't deny it.'

Judith was taken aback, then she said quickly: 'He's marrying you, not her!'

'Because he wants children and she doesn't want any, she said.'

Judith stared at her, appalled. 'She told you that at the party? My God, what a bitch!' No wonder Luke Doulton had looked so angry, no wonder Caroline had been on her way out of his firm within hours.

'She said he only wants me to get himself some sons. He promised his mother that he'd give her grandchildren, Caroline said. He started looking for a suitable wife and I was just the first girl to come along.' Baba frowned, her mouth unsteady. 'Well, that was what she implied, she didn't actually put it like that. She pretended it was a joke at first, she smiled all the time, but she wasn't being funny. She hinted that Luke had been in love with her and would have married her if she had agreed to have children. Luke didn't say a word, he just stood there. I was so embarrassed. Then Luke said something very quietly; I didn't even catch what he said—and she walked away. Even then he didn't deny what she'd said. Someone else arrived and after that he never mentioned her again until he told me she'd left and he'd offered you the job. So you see, you must take it. While I'm in America he might take her back.'

'I doubt that very much,' Judith said drily. Luke Doulton didn't look to her like the sort of man who gives you a second chance; Caroline had destroyed any hopes she had ever had of him. What a fool she must be—or had he already made it clear that their affair was over and she was out of his life anyway?

'Or take on someone else like her,' Baba added, and Judith eyed her sharply.

'You don't seem too sure of him.'

'I was until . . . I don't dare to ask him how much truth there was in what she said, but I can't help wondering. He did ask me if I'd have children right away and he did say his mother was getting impatient because he didn't have any children. I'm not dumb, Judith; I know there have been plenty of other girls in his life. That didn't bother me in the beginning. I thought of them as being in the past, but now I can't help wondering if the future will be the same.'

'Are you saying that you're getting cold feet about marrying him?' Judith was intent now, watching her face and trying to guess at what lay behind her blue eyes. Why had Baba come here tonight to talk to her? Why hadn't she wanted to tell all this to Ruth?

'I'm crazy about him,' Baba confided. 'He sends cold shivers up and down my spine. You must admit, he's terribly sexy, Judith, even if he isn't your type.'

What Baba really meant was that Judith was not Luke's type. Judith's hard-headed realism about herself made it possible for her to smile; she knew she wasn't Luke Doulton's type. He might want to use her brains, but he had no use for her as a woman.

'Please, take that job,' Baba said pleadingly. 'If you're there I'll feel much easier about going away to California, I know you won't be a threat to me, but someone else might.'

'Thanks,' Judith said drily. Baba was too wrapped up in her own problems to be aware of offering any insults; she just looked at Judith with her big blue eyes full of anxiety, and Judith felt horribly sorry for her. 'Are you going to tell him about the screen test before you go?'

Baba hesitated, then shook her head. 'I'll just say I'm going over there to work; he's used to me flying off to model abroad. If I get the part I'll have to tell him, but until then I'd rather keep it to myself. Judith, will you take that job?'

'Probably,' said Judith, and Baba's face lit up with relief.

'You're an angel! Just keep Caroline Rendell away from him—she's not only beautiful, she's clever, and I'm scared of her. Let me know if Luke starts seeing her again—will you? You will, won't you, Judith?'

'You're asking me to spy on him,' Judith said tersely. 'I don't like that idea, Baba. If you don't trust him you shouldn't be marrying him.'

'It isn't him I don't trust, it's her,' explained Baba. She got up, shivering. 'I must go, it's quite chilly tonight, isn't it? Thanks for listening, Judith.'

On the way to the door Judith asked her: 'Why didn't you tell all this to Ruth, by the way?'

'Ruth?' Baba stood still in front of the door. 'She would only worry about me, but you're so self-contained, Judith. Nothing worries you, does it? I could tell you anything and you'd just listen and be very objective. Ruth's too involved; I couldn't talk to her honestly.'

Judith wasn't sure she found that so very complimentary; it made her sound very detached and cold, but then maybe that was how Baba saw her. Baba had always been so happy and carefree, perhaps she didn't want Ruth to see her in any other mood, but it seemed to Judith that Luke Doulton was already putting lines into Baba's smooth, unlined face; he was altering her nature simply by taking over her life. Baba had never been so serious before; Judith couldn't remember seeing her close to tears, openly worried and ill at ease. She was very fond of her, in spite of that old sense of envy because Baba was so stunning. This was a new Baba, and Judith didn't like what was happening to her.

She rang Luke next morning early and told him that she had decided to accept his offer of a job.

'Good,' he said. 'Can you start next Monday?' He didn't sound overjoyed or surprised, but then she hadn't expected him to.

'Yes,' she agreed, deciding to play it as he did. If he could be terse and calm, then so could she.

'I'll have to spend the first morning putting you in the picture,' he said. 'My previous assistant left everything in a mess; there are dozens of loose ends to be picked up. Nine o'clock in my office?'

'Yes.'

'Could you see my legal office this week and work out the small print of your contract with them?'

'I'll make an appointment,' she said, and heard him laugh.

'You're an extraordinary girl,' he said, then he rang

off. Judith looked at the telephone as she replaced it. Isn't that the pot calling the kettle black? she asked him mentally as she walked away.

His legal department moved like greased lightning. Judith spent a morning with them talking over the various clauses; they contacted her own solicitor and on the Friday afternoon the contract was ready to be signed.

She had a date with Robert that Saturday evening. He took her out to dinner and then on to a nightclub to dance. It was the second date they had had that week and Mrs Murry had become quite interested in him. 'Why didn't you bring him here for dinner one evening?' she had suggested, and Judith had made a teasing face at her.

'What are you planning to do? Ask him about his intentions? Come on, Grandma, two dates in a week doesn't mean wedding bells in the offing!'

'Who said it did? I like to meet your friends, that's all.' Her grandmother had pretended to be indignant and Judith had grinned at her.

'You don't fool me—you're a wicked old romantic!'

She liked Robert, but she scarcely knew him yet, she didn't want to build a pleasant friendship into a deathless love affair, nor did she want her grandmother to terrify poor Robert by being so obvious in her matchmaking.

Even so her grandmother had scrutinised her dress that evening, a hopeful look in her eye. 'You look very attractive,' she had told her, and Judith had given her a kiss.

'I know how I look.'

'You underestimate yourself,' Mrs Murry said impatiently. 'I blame your mother. She should never have left you to yourself so much. You're far too distant. You're so used to being on your own that you don't even know what you're missing.'

'Robert's not my first boy-friend, for heaven's sake! I had plenty of fun in New York.' Once she had even taken a boy-friend over to Boston to stay with her mother and stepfather; it had been a disastrous weekend. Her stepfather had been gruff and offhand and her mother had kept on making pointed remarks about weddings, she had got the idea that Judith was about to announce her engagement. Judith had set her right as soon as they were alone, but by then the whole weekend had been a write-off. Judith had been embarrassed, her boy-friend nervous and her stepbrothers so noisy and boisterous that it was impossible to be around them for long without getting a headache. Judith's mother appeared to have a permanent headache, or so she claimed. During her years in New York Judith had seen little of the family; she couldn't help feeling that she was an outsider, she knew her stepfather saw her as one and her mother only looked uneasy whenever Judith was there and friction started.

As she and Robert were dancing that evening she thought that maybe she *would* take him home to meet her grandmother sometime soon. He was one of the nicest men she had met in years, very easy to talk to and full of amusing stories about his travels. By now Judith had discovered that he had, in fact, been married ten years ago but that his wife had died of a rare tropical disease which she had contracted when he took her to India for a holiday. Robert admitted that he had blamed himself for years, he hadn't wanted to marry again. His first marriage had been so happy and so short; it had left him with a bitter sense of loss.

'Are you over it now?' she had asked, watching him with sympathy, and he had nodded, smiling.

'It sometimes seems to me that it happened to someone else—I remember what happened, but I can't actually get that feeling again.' He had paused, then added: 'Thank God. It was bad while it lasted, I wouldn't want to feel like that again. It was like being locked up in a room without windows; I couldn't see or hear anything. I think it was two years before I started being alive again, and I don't remember a damn thing that happened in between.'

Looking at his friendly, cheerful face she couldn't imagine him torn apart by grief, but she didn't doubt his sincerity. The very fact that his pain had been so alien to his usual character must have made it worse for him. That was what worried her about Baba—someone who is sunny and sweet-natured can be more at risk than someone who has already learnt how to absorb pain. Nothing in her life had ever hurt Baba until now; how would she ever cope with it?

The nightclub was dim and shadowy. Tables lined the walls, you could just make out the faces of people sitting at them. The beat of the music throbbed in the small room, lights flashed, multi-coloured and dazzling.

'You don't get migraine, do you?' Robert asked, looking down at her anxiously.

'No, why?'

'These lights can spark off migraine—my wife used to get them . . .' He stopped and grimaced, then drew her closer, his arm a tight band across her back. 'I like your perfume—what is it?' he asked, changing the subject too obviously.

'Patou,' she said. 'Expensive, but it was a present on my last birthday; I've used very little of it, I save it for special occasions.'

'I'm glad you think this is one,' he murmured, his cheek against hers. They moved around the floor in silence for a moment; Judith had her eyes half-closed and for a second she thought she was imagining what she saw, but then she opened her eyes fully and looked hard through the smoky shadows at the couple dancing a little way to the right of them and it *was* Luke Doulton, and the woman in his arms, her head on his shoulder and her arms wound round his neck, *was* Caroline Rendell.

Over Caroline's black head Luke's eyes stared back at Judith with a faintly startled expression in them as though he, too, thought he was seeing things for a moment.

Judith was frozen in shock and mounting anger. Of course it was none of her business, she had no right to be angry, but she was furious. Baba had been absolutely spot on with her doubts and worries about Caroline and Luke; just the sight of them dancing so close that you couldn't have got a thin sheet of paper between them made Judith's teeth meet.

She gave them a last, contemptuous stare as the music stopped and Robert guided her back to their table. A bottle of champagne was waiting for them in a silver ice bucket; Robert poured them each a glass and handed Judith one with a smile.

'Enjoying yourself?' he asked, and she managed to smile back and say she was having a wonderful time. It didn't seem too convincing to her, but in the dim light Robert couldn't see the icy sparkle of her eyes. She sipped the golden wine while Robert told her about a trip to South America he was going to make next month.

'If you fancy seeing Peru . . .' he invited, his eyes warm.

'I'll be back at work by then, thanks all the same.' She found it hard to concentrate on what he was talking about; she was too busy going over and over in her mind the sight of Luke Doulton with the elegant Miss Rendell shackled to him. There had been something desperate about the way those slim arms clung to his neck. Judith almost felt sorry for her; Luke

Doulton really was a first-class bastard! Baba had only flown off yesterday. He hadn't wasted much time, had he? And that was how it would always be, presumably— as soon as he was out of Baba's sight he would have some other woman in his arms.

'With Schewitz and Quayle?' Robert asked.

'No, I'm going to work for Luke Doulton.' Judith's voice was loaded with tension, and Robert picked it up, he peered at her in bewilderment, as well he might; she didn't sound like somebody looking forward to starting a new job, she sounded more like somebody with a hatchet looking for a head to bury it in.

'Luke? Really? Doing what?'

'I'm taking over from Caroline Rendell.' In the office, at any rate, Judith thought, her eyes flicking across the room in search of Luke and Caroline. Some of Caroline's activities were far too personal for any stand-in—she obviously meant to carry on with them herself, although how she could bear to do so when she knew Luke was marrying another girl Judith could not imagine.

'Good heavens!' Robert exclaimed, staggered. 'When was this settled?'

'Legally, yesterday. I signed the contract yesterday morning. Mr Doulton offered me the job last Monday.' She paused and added crisply: 'He works fast.' And that's putting it mildly, she thought.

Robert leaned back, studying her, his champagne glass balanced on the flat of his hand. 'I hope you know what you're doing, Judith. He isn't an easy man to work for, I'm told.'

'I'm sure your informant knew what she was talking about.'

'It was a he, actually,' Robert said mildly. 'Do I get the impression you don't like him much?'

'Like him?' Judith repeated. 'No, I *don't* like him

much.' She felt so much anger and contempt for Luke Doulton that she had to suppress it or she would startle Robert out of his wits. 'Luke Doulton is a . . .'

'Good evening.' The level voice halted the adjectives before they could escape from her tongue and she looked up, stiffening.

'Oh, hallo, Luke,' Robert said hurriedly, pulling himself together rather faster than Judith managed to do. 'I didn't spot you earlier. Just arrived?'

'Not long ago,' Luke said evasively, and Judith wondered how long he and Caroline had been dancing together in that blatant fashion without her noticing them.

What had he done with Caroline? Left her skulking behind a pillar out of sight?

'Is Baba with you?' asked Robert, glancing around the dim room.

'No, I'm with a party of clients who are doing the town before going off to catch their plane.' Luke looked from Robert to Judith. 'I came over to ask you to dance.' He extended his hand and she looked at it as if it was a snake.

'Sorry, I've just sat down and my feet are tired.'

She saw his brows jerk together, his mouth compress, then his hand fastened around her wrist and in one pull yanked her to her feet. 'I want to talk to you,' he said as he gripped her wrist. 'Excuse us, Robert, she'll be back with you in a minute.'

Judith couldn't make a public scene; it wasn't her style. She had no option but to follow him on to the small, crowded floor. He put an arm round her and went on holding her other hand as they began to dance. Judith averted her head, her body rigid in his arm.

'All right, you saw me with Caroline, but you needn't go rushing off to worry Baba with the story, because it wasn't how it looked,' he said in clipped, brusque accents.

'Don't tell me, tell Baba.'

'I want to leave Baba out of it altogether . . .'

'I'm sure you do.' She made no effort to hide her icy contempt and she felt his fingers tighten around her hand until they hurt. Luke Doulton was getting angry, too, but that didn't bother Judith one inch.

'I didn't bring Caroline here tonight,' he went on, she came with somebody else, an old client from Amsterdam. Caroline always sees him when he's in London, so I shouldn't have been surprised when she appeared with him, but there wasn't much I could do about it once she was actually here.'

Judith laughed shortly. 'So to make it clear to her how unwelcome she was, you danced with her cheek to cheek!'

'Look, I don't have to explain myself to you,' he muttered thickly, and even in that dim light she could see the dark colour creeping up his face.

'Who asked you to?'

'What gives you the right to look at me as though I'd broken every one of the ten commandments?' he grated.

'If you don't like the way I look at you the solution is in your hands. Tear my contract up. I wouldn't want to work for you now anyway. Will you take me back to my table? I'm not enjoying myself, and I don't suppose you are.'

'Enjoying myself? You've got to be kidding! I just want your promise that you won't unload all this on to Baba. I've told you the truth. Caroline and my Dutch client have gone now . . .'

'How convenient!'

'My God, who the hell do you think you are?' He drew away and glared down at her; in the shadowy room she saw his grey eyes like hard points of silver light. He was tense and tight-lipped and staring at her as though disbelieving his senses; she got the feeling he had expected he would be able to talk her into believing his version of what had been going on, he hadn't expected her to refuse to listen to him. No doubt Luke Doulton was always listened to and believed, at least to his face. He looked like a man in a new situation; one he did not like at all.

'I'm an old friend of Baba's; that's who I am. You only got engaged to her last week. Tonight you're here with someone else—and don't tell me you and Caroline Rendell were talking business out there on the floor, because I'm not stupid.'

'That's just what you are! You saw me dancing with someone and you're making a Federal case out of it, but you're wrong, you're jumping to conclusions—and anyway, it's all none of your goddamned business. If you go to Baba with this story you'll be doing it because you want to make trouble and for no other reason. You won't be doing Baba any favours. It may give you a kick to interfere, but don't pretend to be so damned righteous about it, because if you do tell her you'll only make her miserable and all over nothing.'

The music ended, Judith broke away from him and walked back to her table and Robert, her mind in confusion. Should she tell Baba? Or was he right? Should she just mind her own business and keep her mouth shut?

Robert looked at her curiously as she sat down. 'What was all that about? It looked from here as though you were having the row to end all rows. I half expected the two of you to come to blows any minute.'

'We were arguing over a matter of principle,' Judith explained. 'Robert, I'm tired—would you mind if we left now?'

He glanced at his watch. 'Nearly one—the time has flown! Sure, I'll get us a taxi.'

Across the room Judith saw Luke Doulton leaving; there were a group of other men with him, that much of his story was obviously true. His companions looked like businessmen who have been having a night out at the end of a business trip, and this was just the sort of place you take people like that to see. It was respectable and safe but gave the illusion of being glamorous and a place to have fun. Judith saw Luke clearly for a moment as he paused in the doorway, the brighter lights in the entrance showing her his hard, angry face. Then he had gone, and she waited for Robert to return with news of their taxi. Whether she told Baba about what had happened or not, she probably didn't have a job to go to on Monday, and she felt very depressed.

CHAPTER FOUR

SHE didn't sleep that night; it infuriated her to lie awake hour after hour, brooding over Luke Doulton and his despicable behaviour. It was the first time a man had ever made her lose any sleep—Judith had never been much of a romantic, even in her teens; her common sense would not permit her to turn insomniac over another human being, and her thoughts now were light years from romance; more murderous than amorous. She kept seeing them out there on that dance floor, their moving bodies half shadow, but Caroline Rendell's strangling arms around Luke's neck and his arms round her waist. He must really think she was stupid if he expected her to believe that cock-and-bull story about a client bringing Caroline along there; she should have laughed in his face when he came out with it—well, she had, in a sense; she had snorted disbelievingly and let him know she didn't believe a single word, but somehow that didn't make her feel any happier. It didn't seem adequate for the rage possessing her; she should have done something more positive, but what? Dim visions of boiling oil and thumbscrews drifted through her tired mind; people in the Middle Ages had had such creative imaginations. They didn't just snort with disbelief when people lied to them; bring out the thumbscrews, they said.

She wanted that job. The more she thought about having to turn it down the more furious she became—it was a chance in a million, not merely from the financial point of view, although the salary was pretty fantastic, but because she would move from comparative obscurity into a key position in one of the big multi-national companies. Working so closely with Luke Doulton she would have far more opportunity to learn and at the same time to influence than she would ever have with Schewitz and Quayle; it was, in fact, the sort of job she might have looked forward to in five or ten years if she had gone on climbing the career ladder in New York. Even then, she would have been lucky to get it, because such places rarely went to women; they were the plum jobs and men usually got them.

A man, of course, would never have acted as she had done that evening. If he had seen Luke with another woman a week after getting engaged to someone else he would merely have grinned and admired his nerve and probably his stamina. He wouldn't have lost his temper and been rude to someone like Luke Doulton, he wouldn't have despised him or, if he had, he wouldn't have been open with his contempt, he would have hidden it and smiled like mad. He would have remembered how much he wanted that job and told himself that it was none of his business what Luke Doulton did; out of sight was out of mind, what the eye didn't see the heart didn't grieve over, and so long as Baba didn't find out she wouldn't get hurt. In these fraught situations a cliché was a great comfort, Judith thought, punching her pillow viciously and wishing it was Luke Doulton's head she was thumping.

It didn't make her feel any better to admit to herself that she had lost her temper or that Luke had been right, it was not her business. She wished to God she had never gone to that nightclub with Robert; she would never have seen Luke with Caroline, none of this would have happened and she would be starting work on Monday without a care in the world. Whatever vague suspicions she had had about Luke she would not have had them confirmed in such a graphic fashion, she wouldn't be asking herself what she was going to do when she saw Baba again; was she going to have to tell her the truth or lie? And—if she lied—how was she going to feel about that?

'You could simply forget it ever happened,' a little voice pointed out, inside her head. Oh, yes? Sounds simple, she retorted to it, but I don't happen to have a wipe-clean memory. From now on every time I see Baba I'm going to remember Luke with that other girl and I'm going to feel embarrassed and uneasy, so before long I'll be avoiding Baba like the plague because merely setting eyes on her is bothering me. And if I do tell her what a kingsize rat Luke Doulton is— Baba will be heartbroken, no doubt, and then *she'll* start avoiding *me* because I make her unhappy and she can't forgive me for telling her what she wishes she'd never known.

No, I'm trapped, she admitted, I can't move in any direction without breaking something, and it's all Luke Doulton's damned fault, the man is a menace!

Sunday dawned bright and clear, the only sounds you could hear were the chirping of birds building nests and the rattle of milk bottles as the milkman slammed them down and went whistling back to his float. Wide-eyed and irritable, Judith lay and listened—as far as she could judge the rest of the street was fast asleep, waiting for their Sunday papers and breakfast in bed. Even her grandmother slept late on a Sunday. Although Judith hadn't slept at all she felt full of frustrated, furious energy. She had to work it off on something, so she had a shower, got dressed and went off to finish decorating her new flat very early, leaving Mrs Murry eating breakfast.

'Will you be back for lunch? I'm only having salad, but I could cook you something,' Mrs Murry said, and Judith shook her head.

'I'll probably work all day; I want to get the flat finished today if I can.'

Her grandmother looked at her with sudden compunction. 'I hope you don't feel I'm pushing you out, Judith. I'm very grateful to you for staying since ... it isn't that I don't want to see you, it's just that I'm not used to sharing my house with another woman. I suppose I'm too old to change my ways; it's a bit much to have to get used to having a strange toothbrush in the bathroom.'

Judith laughed. 'I know what you mean—I often wonder if that accounts for the high divorce rate; people just can't get used to strange toothbrushes in the bathroom.'

Mrs Murry chuckled. 'I know it sounds silly, but ...'

'I know, it's the little things that cause the trouble; I like pop music and you don't, you like soap operas on the TV and I don't. You don't have to explain to me, Grandma. I do understand. I'm used to living on my own now, too, you know.'

Mrs Murry frowned. 'I'm not sure I like the sound of that. It's different at your age, you ought to get married.'

'I'm off,' said Judith, her eyes wry, and left the kitchen with a little wave. She drove to her flat through practically deserted streets; the air was so soft that she had the windows wound right down and felt her hair blowing in the wind and the warmth of the sunshine on her cheek, physical sensations which helped to cool her prickling irritation a little. She still hadn't decided whether or not to appear at Luke Doulton's office next morning; it would be a bit of an anti-climax to walk in as cool as a cucumber after the row they had had, but there was still that contract, very much signed and legal, and bristling with sub-clauses over which the various lawyers had spent a lot of midnight oil.

She set to work as soon as she was in the flat; it only took her a couple of hours to finish the painting, and when she had washed her hands and face afterwards she made herself a cup of coffee and perched on a packing case to drink it while she contemplated what she had done and felt a surge of satisfaction. A few moments later she stiffened in mingled alarm and shock when the doorbell rang violently. She wasn't, somehow, surprised when she opened the door and was confronted by Luke Doulton.

'What do you want?' asked Judith, blocking the doorway. She *was* faintly surprised by what he was wearing; a soft tan leather jacket over a cream polo-necked sweater and casual dark brown cords. Stupidly, she expected him to be wearing formal city clothes every time she saw him but the guy must have some time off from work, and the clothes he was wearing, although casual, were quite obviously expensive. The leather jacket was so smooth it invited you to touch it. Judith, however, refrained, in spite of an instinctive wish to do so; she felt he might misinterpret it if she obeyed her instincts.

'Don't be tiresome, Miss Murry; we have to talk.' He stepped forward, she moved to stop him entering the flat, and they eyed each other warily, impatiently, like duellists about to start fighting.

'How did you know I was here?' she asked.

'I rang your home and your grandmother told me. She seemed to think I was someone called Robert, I'm not sure why.' He knew very well why, his eyes held mockery.

'And you didn't disillusion her,' Judith commented coldly.

'I hate to disillusion anyone,' he said, and she picked up the double meaning and stared back at him in contempt.

'So I've noticed,' she said, and his eyes flashed.

'Look, I'm not discussing my private life on your doorstep.' He picked her up by the waist and carried her into the flat, kicking the door shut with his foot before he put her down.

Very flushed, Judith spat out: 'Get your hands off me!' They were gripping her waist in a vice and she tried to unlock them, slapping his hands down. 'Will you let go?' she yelled as the hands merely tightened.

'Don't lose your temper with *me*,' Luke muttered, his fingers shifting. She felt them brush the underside of her breasts and took a fierce, startled breath. He looked down at her at the sound and for a few seconds they stood there, staring at each other, only inches apart, then Judith wrenched herself free and walked away into the sitting-room. It was a moment before Luke followed her, and by then she was standing at the window, staring out blindly, wondering why her heart was battering against her ribs. Their little fight must have made her breathless, she decided.

Quietly, Luke said: 'Look, last night happened just the way I said it did—I was far from pleased to see Caroline again, but in front of a crowd of people I had to be polite to her.'

'I saw how polite you were!'

'I wasn't able to get out of dancing with her; she'd danced with all the other men. And when she put her arms round my neck what on earth was I supposed to do? Remove them? Make a scene in public? It didn't seem important at the time. It still doesn't—not to me. The only person making a big thing of it is you.'

'Why are you so worried about Baba being told if you don't think it's important?' she asked, swinging to face him. 'You know Baba would be hurt if she knew you were with Caroline last night. I know, too. You seem to forget, I've known Baba for most of my life, her sister is my oldest friend. They both matter to me. You don't, and as for the job—well, no doubt I'll get another, it may not be as good, but at least my next employer won't try to blackmail me . . .'

'Blackmail you?' he broke in, his voice rising. 'Now what are you accusing me of?'

'What else do you call it? You came here this morning to point out to me that if I told Baba what I'd seen I'd lose my job—that's blackmail, in my book.'

'I came here to reason with you,' he denied. 'I agree with you that the fact that you're just going to start working for me is irrelevant, but I still don't like your tone or the accusations you fling around with that expression on your face and that isn't irrelevant. I can't have you talking to me like that in front of people at the office; I'd lose any authority I have. They'd put two and two together and decide you're my latest mistress.'

Judith's mouth opened and stayed open, but nothing came out. He looked at her with grim satisfaction.

'What else do you imagine they'd think? If I let a woman talk to me the way you have been doing there wouldn't be any other explanation—they'd decide in two seconds flat that I was so crazy about you that you could walk all over me.'

Judith still couldn't speak; she was too taken aback, and Luke Doulton watched her flushed face before suddenly laughing.

'Well, at least that shut you up for the moment—I'm glad something can. It could be handy to know that in the future.'

Judith swallowed. 'I thought there wasn't going to be any future for me in your firm.'

'That's something we have to discuss,' he said, and ran his amused eyes over her jeans and old shirt. 'You aren't fit to be seen anywhere respectable,' he told her.

'Never mind, there's someone I want you to meet. Have you got a jacket? If so, grab it and come along.'

Judith stood her ground. 'I don't want to meet Caroline Rendell, thank you.'

Especially looking the way she knew she did at that moment; she could imagine the expression in the other woman's eyes as she stared at Judith's old jeans and the paint-stained shirt. Caroline was aware of her own elegance and chic.

'Did I say it was Caroline? It isn't; it's the most important woman in my life, and I want her to take a look at you and decide whether I should take the risk of leaving you in charge of my most confidential business.'

Judith thought, her brow furrowed. 'Your mother?'

'Very clever, Miss Murry. My mother, the most intelligent woman I know; she could run rings round most of the men who work for me—and has, in the past. My father didn't make a move without consulting her.'

'She wasn't at the engagement party,' Judith thought aloud. 'Didn't she approve of your engagement?'

'Very much so, and she liked Baba. I took Baba down to meet her—don't tell me you didn't know that? I thought Baba told you everything.' His eyes mocked and Judith smiled wryly.

'Then why didn't she come to the party? Doesn't she live in London?'

'She's very frail, she can't travel far, it tires her too much. She lives in Kent, it won't take us more than three quarters of an hour to get there and we can have lunch at the house.'

Judith looked down at herself. 'I can't meet your mother looking like this, I'll have to go home and change first.'

Luke looked at his watch. 'How long would that take you? It's eleven now. Can you change quickly?'

'Give me ten minutes,' said Judith, and he grimaced.
'I don't believe in miracles; no woman can be ready
in ten minutes.'

'Try me.'

He contemplated her with his head on one side, his
face amused. 'I've never met a woman like you,' he said.
'I believe you *will* do it in ten minutes, if only to prove
me wrong. Well, come on—don't just stand there!'

It wasn't until they were almost at her grandmother's
house that Judith realised she had left her own car
parked outside the flats. It was locked and would be
safe enough there, but it showed her with disturbing
clarity how Luke Doulton could get his own way,
because she hadn't stopped to think about her car, she
had let him hustle her out of her flat and into his fast
red sports car without the faintest hint of an argument.
He had taken her by surprise with his demand that she
should come and meet his mother. She couldn't deny
that she wanted to meet Mrs Doulton; she was curious
about her. What Luke had said about his mother
hadn't been entirely new to her; she had heard
something of Mrs Doulton when she was in New York,
she knew that Mrs Doulton was English and had
married her husband when he was working for a year in
London and that after his death she had returned to
live in England for most of the year, only visiting her
children at odd intervals. The Doulton legend had
involved her; she was supposed to have been the power
behind the throne, people said that her husband had
always consulted her about his deals, but she had kept
out of the limelight and acted in private. Only those
who visited the Doulton home on Rhode Island ever
met her, and of those people only a few ever got
invitations to her other house, the one in very isolated,
wooded country in Vermont, with a view of lakes and
fields below it, but anyone who did visit the family

there boasted about it to their friends and acquaint-
ances. Judith had heard her name mentioned with awe;
yet nobody had seemed to know much about Mrs
Doulton, which only increased her legendary status.

Luke parked outside the house and looked at his
watch again. 'Right—you've got ten minutes,' he said.
'Any chance of a cup of coffee while I wait?'

'Of course, come in.' Judith let herself into the house
with him on her heels and Mrs Murry came out of the
kitchen with a cucumber in her hand and a surprised
expression on her face.

'Oh, hello, he found you, then,' she said, and smiled
past Judith at the man with her. 'I'm very pleased to
meet you at last, Robert, are you going to have lunch
with us? I'm afraid it's only salad, but I'm sure I can
find a tin of something to go with it. I've been telling
Judith to bring you to lunch for ages, I only wish I'd
had more warning, but so long as you don't mind pot
luck . . .'

'He isn't Robert,' explained Judith when she could
get a word in edgeways, and Mrs Murry stared at Luke
in surprise. 'Grandma, this is Luke Doulton. Mr
Doulton, my grandmother, Mrs Murry.'

Mrs Murry peered at Luke as he strolled forward,
offering his hand. For a second Judith thought her
grandmother was going to offer him the cucumber, then
she switched it to another hand and gave Luke the right
one to shake, smiling.

'I'm sorry! I thought you were Judith's young man.'

'Perfectly natural, I'm very glad to meet you, Mrs
Murry, I've heard so much about you.'

'Have you?' Mrs Murry looked at Judith. 'I'm afraid
I can't return the compliment; I could have sworn
Judith was going out with someone called Robert.'

'I am—and Mr Doulton isn't my young man, he's my
new boss. I'm going up to change into some clean

clothes—could you make him a cup of coffee, Grandma? I won't be ten minutes.' Judith was embarrassed, mainly by Luke Doulton's smile rather than her grandmother's confusion. She ran upstairs, leaving Mrs Murry to deal with Luke.

She stripped off her jeans and shirt, washed quickly, chose a dark red wool dress from her wardrobe and was dressed and brushing her hair when Mrs Murry tapped at the door five minutes later. 'Come in,' Judith said as the door opened. She looked at her grandmother with a smile. 'I was just coming down.'

'Did you want some coffee?'

'I haven't got time; Mr Doulton's in a hurry. Did he tell you we were going to have lunch at his mother's house?'

'Yes. He's charming, isn't he? And so handsome—I can't remember when I last met such an attractive man. I had to put my glasses on to look at him properly— such an unusual colour, his hair. What colour would you call it? Mahogany?'

'Brown,' said Judith, giving her own reflection a quick check. She looked calm and neat and that was all she could say for herself, but that was precisely the image she wanted to give Mrs Doulton. She got up and Mrs Murry followed her down the stairs, telling her far too loudly: 'Couldn't you have found something prettier than that dress?'

Luke Doulton loomed in the hallway, and Judith could tell he had been eavesdropping. He was smiling; she was beginning to recognise the variations on his smiles and this one was his teasingly amused smile, it was probably the one she liked least of all of them.

'Ten minutes exactly,' he said. 'Only just made it, though.'

'Pedant,' Judith murmured, picking up her suede jacket. She was aware of her grandmother looking at him hard. Turning, she kissed her on the cheek. 'I won't be late,' she said.

'Definitely mahogany,' Mrs Murry told her. 'I can't imagine why you say brown.'

As they drove away from the house Luke asked curiously: 'What's mahogany?' and Judith said: 'Oh, nothing,' her eyes on the driving mirror, watching a car pulling out behind them.

'Where exactly does your mother live?' she asked, settling into the comfortable leather seat with a sigh. It was a beautiful morning for a drive into the country, much more enjoyable than working in her flat. She considered the sight of Luke Doulton's long-fingered hands on the steering wheel; they suggested a sensitivity and strength which did not fit with what she had learnt about him so far. Well, she corrected herself, the strength maybe—but she hadn't seen many signs of sensitivity as yet.

'Just outside Canterbury, a tiny village called Lambourne—on the motorway we should make it there well before lunch.'

'Is she expecting you?'

'I rang her this morning.' He turned his head, the thick hair whipping across his forehead, and smiled at her. 'She's expecting you, too—I told her I'd bring you even if I had to manhandle you to get you there.'

'Oh, did you?' Judith's voice held cool hauteur, but it only made him laugh; he was not an impressionable man, she decided, the only way you might be sure of making an impression on him was to use a hammer. He was too used to having his own way, he had had too much money and too much power at an early age and had been answerable to no one but himself all these years; it had made him as impervious as a steel wall.

'Did Baba tell you I'd been dating Caroline before I

met Baba?' he asked suddenly, and Judith looked round at him, her eyes wide and startled.

'Yes; she told me what Caroline had said to her at the party, too. Not a very pleasant girl, is she? She upset Baba on what should have been a wonderful evening.'

'I wonder what else Baba has told you,' he mused, half to himself. 'You make me nervous, Miss Murry. You have a horrible habit of saying what you think and damn the consequences. It can be unnerving. I'm amazed you've made it as far as you have in banking, that sort of habit usually gets you into trouble. You must have had a very tolerant boss.'

'John never did anything I disapproved of,' Judith told him.

'How wise of him; who did the embalming?'

'What?' She looked round, baffled, then saw his teasing smile again and relaxed. 'Oh, very funny.' But, in a sense, he had hit the nail on the head. John had been slightly stuffy, totally devoted to his work and scrupulously conscientious, a very admirable man, but she had to admit—slightly stuffy. Her gaze travelled to the wing mirror on her side of the car and she saw the vehicle which had pulled out behind them when they left London still firmly in place, glued to their tail. Judith frowned. She stared at the two men in the front seat; they wore dark glasses, you couldn't see much of their faces, but their shoulders had a bulk under their jackets which made them fairly menacing, not men you would like to run into on a dark night. She looked at the scenery flashing past. They had been driving for a good twenty minutes now and it might be a coincidence that that car was still behind them after what must be around twenty miles through the suburbs of London, but Judith had very little faith in coincidence.

'I don't want to sound alarmist, but we're being followed,' she said to Luke Doulton. 'Look in your mirror—that blue car has been there for miles and it never budges; I'm certain it's following us.'

He looked obediently into his mirror, she saw his dark brows wing upwards and flushed.

'I'm not imagining it! Now that we've hit the motorway put on some speed and just see if they fall back—I bet they don't. You must be insane driving around alone in an ordinary car, you know. You must be at risk, someone in your position. I realise you must feel much safer over here than you do in the States, you aren't such a public figure in Britain, but you really should be more careful. You've even put the top down on this car, haven't you? You're a sitting duck in an open car. I know you must enjoy being able to relax and act as though you were just like everybody else now and again, but it isn't wise, even in Britain. Those men back there could be anything from kidnappers to assassins.' She stopped talking because Luke was looking at her with laughter in his eyes. Judith stared at him in disbelief, then went rigid as he put his hand on her knee.

He took his hand away almost at once, though, after giving her knee a paternal pat. 'Thanks for the concern, but those assassins back there are on my payroll. What is it you call them over here? Minders, isn't it? Well, those guys are my minders. They're security men, and you're quite right, I would be a fool if I didn't take precautions, but I prefer to ignore my minders when I get the chance. That's why they're in that car back there and I'm here with you, which is a much more enjoyable experience.'

'Oh, hell!' Judith muttered with force. 'Why did you let me make a fool of myself? Why didn't you tell me right away?'

'It was sweet of you to take such an interest in my welfare,' he said, grinning, and she could have hit him.

'And I was impressed by your powers of observation; I must tell those guys to be less obvious in future. They're supposed to be discreet; if events did take a nasty turn their arrival unexpectedly could make all the difference. I rely on the element of surprise.'

'I'll remember that,' said Judith. She was learning a lot about him very quickly; some of it was surprising, but all of it was very illuminating. Was that how Luke timed his raids on unsuspecting companies—discreet observation from a distance followed by a surprise swoop out of the blue? Very effective, no doubt, and difficult to fight him off once he had arrived, you wouldn't know for a while what had hit you.

Just before they reached Canterbury he turned off on a narrow road which meandered away across the Kent countryside with low hedges on each side and beyond them grassy fields full of black and white cows and elms just coming into leaf; in the orchards in the distance pink blossom made a lacy pattern on the blue sky and beyond the swaying blossom she saw the white cowls of a pair of oasthouses. Luke slowed as they approached a pair of open gates; he swooped through them and headed down a drive bordered with lime trees. The blue car followed and parked at the end of the drive, a stone's throw from the black and white timbered Elizabethan house in front of which Luke had halted.

'Damsels,' he said to Judith; leaning his folded arms across the wheel and watching her as she stared at the house with delight. 'Originally it was called Damsel's Piece, according to the earliest deeds—probably because it was given to somebody's daughter when she got married, a sort of dowry, I suppose. Some time in the eighteenth century they dropped the word Piece and just called it Damsels. My mother has a theory that it was the land which was the dowry, not the house—the house came later.'

She was barely listening; her eye following the crooked line of the roofs, wavy and spotted with green moss, the pink tiles faded by time to a gentle rose. Barley-sugar chimneys twisted upwards; the windows were diamond-latticed, the black beams wandering like the road on which Luke had just driven, the house had a stubborn eccentricity as though determined to draw attention to the fact that it was a remarkable survival from a less uniform age, and the gardens surrounding it were laid out in period with low box hedges around the lush green lawns, yew trees trimmed into shapes here and there and in the distance a little wicker arbour overhung with climbing roses and ivy.

'How romantic!' Judith sighed, looking beyond the garden to the small park which stretched away to a belt of trees on one side and on the other to an obviously ancient red brick wall. 'What a dreamy place; has your mother lived here long?'

'Let me see—nearly ten years now, I suppose. She used to know the people who owned it years ago and when she heard it was on the market she rushed over to buy it at once. She was in love with it when she was just a little girl, I think; she said it was her great dream to live here.'

'I'm not surprised—it's that sort of house, it has magic.'

He smiled. 'I've a strong feeling you and my mother are going to get on like a house on fire! Come in and meet her. She'll have heard the car, nothing happens here that she doesn't know about, she'll be waiting for us.'

Judith got out of the car and then saw that the front door stood open and an old woman was walking slowly to meet them. She was tall and very thin with snow-white hair and a wrinkled, sallow face; her dark blue dress blew about in the wind and she hunched her shoulders against it with a cross frown. Judith stared, thinking; no, his mother is nothing like him at all—but then did I really expect to see an immediate resemblance?

'Midday, you said, Luke! That means twelve o'clock to me, I don't know what time you call this, but the clock just struck one and I set that clock by Big Ben on the News at Ten every night, so I know it isn't wrong. If you're going to arrive at one, you should say so and not be so vague. It's very thoughtless of you. We've been very fidgety for the last hour, I can tell you; my legs have almost worn down to the anklebone running up and down stairs to say there hasn't been a phone call and you haven't crashed the car or been hijacked and taken off to South America in a laundry basket. When you specify a time, you should stick to it. If the lamb is ruined don't blame me, you only have yourself to blame!' Without drawing breath she turned and stared at Judith, demanding: 'Who's this, then? That's not your fiancée, she had fair hair. You didn't say you were bringing someone with you, is she staying for lunch? I don't know if there's enough.'

'Of course there is, Fanny,' said Luke, quite unperturbed by the scolding. He kissed her cheek. 'How are you? You look well. I'm sorry we're late, I hope the lamb isn't uneatable. This is Miss Murry, my new personal assistant.'

Judith offered her hand rather nervously under the penetrating stare the old woman gave her. Without taking it Fanny turned and stumped away towards the house, leaving Judith with the realisation that in Fanny's eyes guests did not shake hands with housekeepers. Luke gave her a rueful grin.

'Fanny has been looking after my mother for years, I don't know what my mother would do without her,' he said in a voice pitched loud enough to reach the departing Fanny's ears.

'Lunch will be ten minutes—and you've got to go up and see your mother before you sit down at the table, so don't dawdle,' the old woman flung over her shoulder, ignoring his flattery. Judith found it suddenly very funny, but when she looked down, smiling to herself, Luke gripped her arm, muttering: 'One day your sense of humour is going to get you into trouble!'

She looked down at the hand curled around her forearm. 'One day you're going to get a kick on the shins if you keep grabbing me like that!'

'Charm itself, aren't you?' he said drily, but he removed the hand, adding: 'You can come up with me and meet my mother right away. Keep that expression on your face—that's the one I want her to see; it would curdle milk at forty paces!'

Judith immediately assumed an angelic smile, dark eyes wide and innocent. 'This one?' she asked, and Luke gave her a strange, intent stare before which her eyes fell instinctively, although she had no idea why they should.

CHAPTER FIVE

SHE wasn't sure, afterwards, exactly what she had been expecting to see when she followed Luke into the large, sunlit bedroom, but it certainly had not been the vision she did see, sitting up against banked pillows, watching the door as they came through it. Mrs Doulton was beautiful. That was Judith's first thought—a flash of realisation which came with a jab of sharp surprise. Her second thought came hard on the heels of the first; beautiful? she asked herself, staring, was that the right word to describe someone who was obviously almost sixty and so thin and frail that as you looked at her you felt a pang of anxiety?

'Luke, you're so late—I was worried!'

'You shouldn't have been.' Luke sat on the edge of the bed and took the hand his mother held out to him; it was engulfed in his long fingers, Mrs Doulton's skin looked impossibly white against the hard brown strength of her son's large hand.

Judith waited and a moment later Mrs Doulton looked past Luke, smiling, and at once Judith saw the beauty again and this time knew where it came from—this was not a beauty you could pin down to any one feature. It was not in the wide-open grey eyes or the small delicately formed nose or the pale mouth. It was in that smile, that eagerness and radiance, in the impression of luminosity—Mrs Doulton was so insubstantial that the mind inside the body had become what you saw and reacted to, the physical shell so worn down that her inner light shone through it visibly.

Luke glanced round and got up. 'Mother, this is Judith Murry—Judith, my mother.'

Judith quickly went over to take the hand Mrs Doulton held out. 'Sit down, Judith, it's good of you to give up your Sunday to come and see me—I hope Luke didn't bully you into it.'

'Not much,' said Judith, sitting down, and Mrs Doulton looked surprised and then laughed.

'Careful, Mother, she has an annoying habit of telling the truth,' Luke warned in a dry voice.

'That must be a new experience for you, darling,' Mrs Doulton told him, giving him an amused look, then she asked Judith: 'You've just got back from New York, I hear; how was it?'

'Noisy,' said Judith, smiling. 'Electrifying and exciting—but it must be one of the noisiest cities on earth, and very disorientating, because they keep pulling it down and building it up again overnight. Nothing ever satisfies them, I suppose; they always think they can make it bigger and better. I don't know why they bothered to send spaceships to the moon— sooner or later the skyscrapers of Manhattan are going to get there anyway!'

Mrs Doulton laughed, watching her intently and making Judith nervous and very aware of her own shortcomings. Luke's mother had only recently met Baba—Judith must be something of an anti-climax after that, in her very plain dark red dress with her windblown hair tossed around her thin, sallow face. Judith looked down, flushing; the brief vivacity extinguished in her the moment she remembered what she actually looked like. Mrs Doulton, like Baba, must have been a real knock-out when she was young if even at sixty she could make you believe she was still beautiful.

'Don't loom, Luke,' Mrs Doulton ordered. 'We don't

need you—go down and coax Fanny into a better mood; she's very cross because you were late.'

'You shouldn't have got worried; Fanny only gets cross because you're upset, you know that.'

'I know everything there is to know about Fanny, thank you, and I can't help getting agitated when you're nearly an hour late.' Mrs Doulton waved an imperious hand at him. 'Go down and talk to her!'

Luke went out and his mother gave Judith a rueful smile. 'Stupid of me to fret over him at his age, a habit I picked up in the States—such a violent society especially when money is involved. His father had several narrow scrapes—I lived in terror for weeks when someone with a grudge against him threatened to have him killed!'

'Luke has his security men on hand all the time, I gather, even over here—so I shouldn't worry too much.' Judith hesitated, then told her about the little incident on the way down to Lambourne. Mrs Doulton listened and laughed.

'Were you scared?'

'Petrified,' Judith admitted. 'I felt so silly when he told me they were his own men; I'd been trying to work out how to escape them!'

Mrs Doulton lay back, her thin hands immobile on the sheet. 'You aren't what I was expecting,' she said suddenly, and Judith looked at her warily.

'What had you been expecting?' Had Mrs Doulton expected someone like Caroline Rendell? An elegant, beautiful woman with charm as well as brains? Instantly, Judith felt both irritated and depressed; why were looks so important? She had felt she was getting on very well with Luke's mother, yet Mrs Doulton, too, was measuring her against that implacable standard and finding her unimpressive simply because she was not beautiful.

'Luke told me you were prickly and difficult,' Mrs Doulton said, taking her by surprise. 'I gather you argue with him all the time; he says you're obstinate and too free with your opinions.'

'Oh, did he?' Judith murmured, her dark eyes lowered to hide the rebellious glint in them. So that was what he had told his mother, was it? Had he told her *why* she had been free with her opinions? Did Mrs Doulton know about him and Caroline Rendell?

Almost on cue, Mrs Doulton asked her: 'Have you met your predecessor, Miss Rendell?'

'Yes,' said Judith with what she hoped was commendable discretion and lack of intonation, keeping her gaze down because she knew it would betray her.

'She's exactly the type of girl Luke has had working for him in the States; to get on over there you need that sort of gloss, she can be so charming and she dresses perfectly, she looks the part.'

'Yes,' said Judith through almost closed lips.

'But her eyes give her away,' Mrs Doulton went on, surprising her into looking up. 'They do, you know,' Luke's mother added, then laughed teasingly, 'Is that why you wouldn't look at me just now? Afraid of what I'd see in your eyes?'

Judith didn't say anything but she laughed back, her face lightening.

'Yes, you can make your mouth smile obediently, you can lie like a trooper, but your eyes tell the truth, and Caroline Rendell has cold eyes,' Mrs Doulton said.

She pushed back a straying strand of the fine hair which looked like silver-gilt wire; had her hair been blonde or red? She wore it in a loose mass tied back behind her head with a pink ribbon; it gave her the fleeting appearance of girlhood except that it was all silver, and so fine now that you could see her pink scalp through it here and there. She was wearing a delicate dusting of powder on her face, the merest brush of pale pink lipstick; a concession to beauty she did not need because her real beauty lay inside her.

'I was taken aback when you came in with Luke,' she said. 'Taken aback and delighted—I can talk to you; I could never talk to Caroline. Luke has told you that one of your chores will be to keep me informed of what he's doing? I don't mean where he is, that sort of thing—he always rings me several times a week whether he's in Tokyo or Los Angeles. I meant as far as the company in London is concerned. I like to know what's going on; I may be stuck in this bed, but that doesn't mean my brain has turned to mashed potato. I keep abreast of current affairs, read the papers each morning, talk to my broker and my banker. The day I stop taking an interest in the rest of the world I'll know I'm dead!'

Judith laughed, very amused and interested. Mrs Doulton looked delicate and finely balanced, but she talked in a direct, frank way that Judith could relate to immediately. There was a toughness in her which she had handed on to her son; it was that core of her which you sensed as soon as you met her, you felt that she had been through great pain and loss and come out strengthened by it and without bitterness. Was it her illness which gave her that strength? Or the death of her husband? It was probably both, Judith decided; life didn't stop handing you problems simply because you had managed to cope with one painful situation, surely? You still had to go on and face new challenges, or was there a time when you emerged on to a plateau of calm and acceptance? No, she thought, watching the other woman's face; that was not the resignation of someone who has stepped out of life, those eyes were still looking outwards,

Mrs Doulton was right about that. She was still very much involved in the world.

'You are an old friend of Baba's, Luke tells me,' Mrs Doulton said, and Judith nodded.

'I've known her for years. Her sister is my best friend.'

'I was beginning to think Luke would never get married. He's been so busy since his father died and he took over.' Mrs Doulton laughed ruefully. 'Oh, there have been girls in his life, but none of them stayed around for long, they never seemed to matter to him; it worried me. He gave all his attention to his work; that was what he really cared about, there was no room in his life for marriage. When a man gets used to living like that it becomes a habit; they get selfish, they don't want to change.' She looked at Judith thoughtfully. 'You're not planning to get married yet?'

'No,' said Judith, unwilling to discuss herself.

Mrs Doulton considered her for a moment, then went on: 'I took to Baba on sight; she's a delightful girl, very sweet and warm, but . . .' She stopped, and Judith frowned, wondering what she had been about to say. Mrs Doulton shrugged, staring towards the window. 'Well, she's what Luke wants and I want him to be happy, one can never guess what goes on inside someone else even when it is your own son.' She turned back to Judith. 'Is Baba what she seems?'

The question was so sudden and so direct that Judith did not answer for a beat of time, she stared, open-eyed, then she smiled. 'Baba is one hundred per cent genuine, believe me. Ruth and I used to wish she wasn't quite so nice, in fact. We were rather jealous of her when she was younger; she was so staggeringly beautiful people used to stare when she went past. We would have liked her to be spiteful or mean, but she never was, she's pure gold all the way through.'

Mrs Doulton listened, watching her, nodding. 'I'm glad I wasn't wrong about her. I'd have been furious if she'd taken me in . . .' Her eyes were self-deriding. 'Isn't it odd how much we dislike being fooled by someone?'

'Not odd at all; who enjoys being made a fool of?'

'Has anyone ever made a fool of you, Judith?'

'Probably, but I can't remember it now—self-protection, I suppose.'

They both laughed, then Mrs Doulton asked: 'How did you get into banking?' and for the next few minutes they talked about more general subjects. Judith found it stimulating and enjoyable; she soon realised that Mrs Doulton had a brain like a knife and an encyclopaedic knowledge of international finance. When Luke came back and told them that lunch was now ready Judith was quite reluctant to stop talking to his mother, she couldn't remember when she had met anyone so interesting or so amusing; Mrs Doulton seemed to have met everyone who mattered in that world of money and her judgments on them were usually coolly accurate without being unkind.

'Come up and see me before you leave, Judith,' Mrs Doulton told her as she followed Luke out of the room, and she looked back, smiling, to nod.

'She likes you,' Luke said drily; she wondered if he was disappointed.

'I hope she does—I liked her a lot.' Judith wondered if she had been through a test which all his personal assistants had to pass. Did he use his mother as litmus paper? An acid test which he regarded as a final judgment?

'A pity I was told to get out, I have a suspicion you didn't show my mother the claws you keep using on me,' he commented, opening a door from the hall and standing back to let her enter the room into which it led, a sunny dining-room with oak-panelled walls whose golden wood gleamed in the light and reflected the bowls of flowers which stood everywhere and filled the air with spring fragrance.

Judith didn't rise to that remark, and as they began eating the delicious lunch which Fanny served them a few moments later, Luke said: 'What do I have to say to make you accept that I wasn't cheating on Baba last night?'

Judith took a mouthful of home-made celery soup, swallowed it while she thought about the question, then looked up and said: 'I'm surprised you take my opinion so seriously; does it matter what I think?'

'I've been asking myself that ever since last night,' he said wryly. 'I don't know why it should, but it does—yes. It may be childish of me, but I have an irrational dislike of being found guilty when I'm innocent.'

'For once?' Judith mocked, laughing at him, and suddenly realising that she actually believed him now; perhaps because of his insistence of innocence and perhaps because she had somehow got to know him much better over the last twenty-four hours.

'Okay, for once,' he said with rueful amusement. 'I've no intention of starting off my marriage by cheating, and it wouldn't be with Caroline, if I was going to stray.'

'No?' Judith queried, still amused. 'Who, then?'

He poured some of the cool golden Muscadet into her glass, his hand steady. 'You, maybe.'

Judith stiffened. 'Don't start flirting with me, Mr Doulton. That's not my scene, I don't steal men from my friends and, even if I did, you're the last man I'd pick. We don't live in the same world.'

'Funny, I'd have said that that was exactly what we did—not many women can talk as shrewdly and intelligently about money as you, and if they can they rarely have a sense of fun or eyes that laugh when they're looking down—or didn't you think I'd noticed that you look down to laugh from time to time?'

Judith flushed, looking down now, not to laugh, but to hide the disturbed expression of her eyes. 'Are you sure you're serious about Baba?' she asked with biting emphasis.

He didn't answer, and they were silent as Fanny removed their soup plates and served the lamb and new potatoes and peas with mint sauce. She talked to Luke scoldingly about his mother as she moved around the table and Luke listened and nodded; patience in his face. He gave her more respect than he ever gave Judith; had she been his nanny? Judith wondered. She behaved like some member of the family.

When they were drinking their coffee later, Luke asked: 'Do you play croquet?' and Judith shook her head, her face surprised.

'I'll teach you, then; there's an old croquet set in the garden shed. I enjoy a game on a fine afternoon; there's something relaxing about it. When my mother first moved here and I unearthed the croquet mallets I hunted out a book on the rules; all I could remember of them was that Alice played it in Wonderland with flamingoes for mallets.'

'I hated *Alice* when I was a child; I thought it was weird and boring.'

'I enjoyed it very much the last time I read it; maybe it isn't a children's book at all. Maybe you have to be grown-up to read it.'

'I haven't read it since I was ten,' Judith confessed.

'You ought to take another look at it; it may surprise you. Coming out to play croquet?'

She got up. 'If you like.' She didn't expect to enjoy herself, but to her surprise she did; they laughed a lot and Luke cheated abominably, quite openly, admitting he liked to win no matter how he bent the rules.

'Sounds ominous,' Judith commented, and he looked down at her, his eyes mocking and brilliant in the late afternoon sunlight. She had a strange swimming sensation; she was dizzy and the back of her neck went cold as though she was going to faint. She must have played too long out in the sun, bending down all the time to tap her ball towards the croquet hoop.

Before they left Luke took her up to say goodbye to his mother, who said: 'Keep in touch, won't you, Judith? I enjoyed our little chat; perhaps when you're at a loose end some day you'll come down again? While Luke's away I'd be glad if you'd ring me every so often when you have time.'

Judith promised. On the way back to London Luke said: 'Tomorrow sharp at nine?' His voice was casual, but she knew he wasn't quite sure of her answer because she felt him watching her sideways.

'I'll be there,' she said calmly. She felt Luke relaxing in his seat. He had the hood up now, the air was cooler with the sun sinking in the sky and a little spring wind blowing through the trees. Judith watched the pink glow on the western heights of the downs where sheep grazed on the short grass and the black shadows thronged in the woods; a late thrush sang defiance to the approaching night and in the little villages in the Weald, in front of them, the lights were springing up like glow-worms in the dusk. Neither she nor Luke talked for some time. Judith felt peaceful and strangely happy; the day which had begun so badly was ending with very different feelings.

By the time Luke pulled up outside her grandmother's house it was almost dark and the street lights were on. Judith undid her seat-belt and looked round at him.

'I enjoyed my day. Thank you.'

'My pleasure,' he said, his face serious. It was stupid, but she suddenly felt uneasy and nervous; she had to get away, she had no idea why.

'Well, goodnight,' she said, scrambling out of the car so fast that she laddered her tights. She got into the house and only when the door was shut behind her did she stop breathing hard; she felt as though she had been menaced by something in that car, her heartbeat was uneven and her face very hot. She was furious with herself for behaving like a schoolgirl on a first date. Luke must think she was kooky; she had bolted as though he'd just grown fangs, and the poor man hadn't so much as laid a finger on her. She must be crazy to let her imagination run away with her like that. For a second she had been convinced he was about to kiss her; she had really felt as though any minute . . . she ran up to her own room and looked at herself in the mirror accusingly.

'Make a pass at you? You wish! As if he would! You need certifying, do you know that? You're out of your mind!' Her dark eyes glittered with self-derision.

Downstairs she heard her grandmother calling. 'Judith? Is that you?'

'Yes, I'll be down in a minute,' Judith called back, and went into the bathroom and shut the door. This time she avoided looking at mirrors; she washed her hands vigorously as though washing away the memory of her own stupidity and a moment later was able to look cool and cheerful before going down to see Mrs Murry.

She arrived at the huge office block next morning in a stream of other employees and had to queue for the lift. It was raining outside, a light spring rain which would probably clear up by noon—or so everyone kept telling each other around her. Judith was nervous and hoped it didn't show. Although Luke had talked to her about what he would expect her to do she was under no illusions about the difficulty of the job; she was going to need all her powers of concentration and every ounce of intelligence she possessed. She already realised that Luke Doulton wasn't the type of man to be ultra-patient; he would probably let her make the odd mistake, but there would be a time limit on how long he expected her to take to get used to the work.

His office was on the top floor and she was the only occupant left in the lift when it reached that level. She stepped out and walked with as much calm as she could to the receptionist seated at a desk in the carpeted lobby.

The girl looked up, smiling. She had a round, smooth-skinned, vivacious face and friendly blue eyes. Judith smiled back. 'Good morning, I'm Judith Murry. I have an appointment . . .'

'With Mr Doulton—yes, Miss Murry, I'll let him know you're here.' With another smile the girl spoke into the intercom and then stood up. 'Will you come this way, Miss Murry? I'll take you to Mr Doulton's office.'

She led the way to a pair of double doors at the end of the lobby, tapped and opened one door. 'Miss Murry, sir.' She stood back to let Judith pass her and then said: 'Shall I make some coffee, sir?'

'In half an hour, Dora,' said Luke, standing up behind a wide desk littered with papers. The door closed and he came forward, pointing to a chair in front of the desk. 'Sit down, Judith. We have a lot to do and very little time to spare.'

She sat down, crossing her legs, and felt him observing the movement, his narrowed gaze increasing her wariness. Luke perched on the edge of the desk, his knee inches from her own. He was wearing his formal city clothes today, but he had tugged his tie loose and his top shirt button was unfastened. She saw the brown, smooth skin of his throat behind the crisp white material and looked away, irritated with herself for the little jab of awareness. This had to stop; he was going to marry Baba, he wasn't free, and if he was, Judith wouldn't be the sort of girl he would look at twice.

'You look very efficient today,' he said, a dry note in his voice.

She looked up again; a flare of pink colour in her face. She was wearing a dark grey woollen suit over a pearl-buttoned white shirt; it gave a touch of chic to her slender figure, she had chosen it quite deliberately to look calm and efficient, and it infuriated her to see from his smile that he guessed at her reasons for wearing it today.

'Right,' Luke said abruptly, handing her a folder. 'Here's a brief synopsis of the work Caroline was handling—you'll have to hunt out the detailed files from her office later, but this will give you a general idea.'

She opened the folder and looked down the typed sheets, her eye moving rapidly. Luke watched her, she wished he would not sit so close, he was distracting her and making it hard to concentrate.

'Take a close look at Sheet 3—those are the companies I'm keeping a watchful eye on and might want to acquire under the right conditions,' he said, and as she slowed down to read the short paragraphs on that page Luke got up and came round behind her. She felt him grasp the back of her chair and lean over. His face almost touched her cheek, she heard his level breathing. Of course he had no idea what he was doing; why should it enter his head that she had suddenly become aware of him? She was human, she thought impatiently; what woman working in such close proximity to any man could be totally unaware of him sexually? Her instincts worked the same as those of any woman, and Luke Doulton was a particularly attractive man; his sexuality was not easy to ignore. She wished to

God she *could* just ignore him. Until yesterday she hadn't dreamt that she would find it so hard to shut out her own femininity and forget that Luke was around, it hadn't occurred to her that there was any danger to her in accepting that job with him. This sort of problem had never arisen before, although she had often worked with attractive men, she had even dated them in her free time on occasions, without having her concentration on work disturbed. She had always found it a simple matter to separate her working and her leisure hours, she enjoyed both without taking the attitudes of one into the performance of the other.

To her relief Luke straightened and walked round behind his desk to sit down. 'When you've absorbed that stuff we'll discuss it,' he said. 'Then we'll have that coffee.'

Judith breathed more calmly. She read through Sheet 3 again and then went on to study the other sheets, before looking up, questions already forming on her lips.

When Luke looked at his watch and said: 'Time for lunch now,' she was amazed because she had long ago ceased to notice the passage of time; she barely recalled the arrival of the coffee or the two phone calls which had interrupted them as they talked. He saw her face and laughed. 'Lost track of the time? So did I until I started to feel hungry. We'll eat quickly in the directors' dining-room and come straight back to finish the discussion, shall we?' It was a rhetorical question; he had it planned that way and she meekly accepted it.

'Want to go to the cloakroom first?' he suggested, walking to the door. 'I'll join you in the lobby in two minutes.'

They were the only occupants of the small dining-room which, Luke told her, was only used occasionally. They had melon and then salad and cold meat followed by cheese and coffee. Judith felt nervous; she said very little now that they had stopped talking about work, it was the only subject which made her feel safe.

'Oh, I forgot,' said Luke, as they walked back to his office. 'I've got something for you.' He opened a drawer in his desk and pulled out a blue leather bound book and tossed it to her.

Catching it, Judith glanced at the title, her face puzzled, then smiled. 'Oh, *Alice* . . .'

'Don't forget to read it,' he said, swivelling in his chair with his hands linked behind his dark brown head. The rain had cleared, as predicted, and the sun was shining through the great plate glass windows lining the wall behind him. Her eyes were dazzled, she stared at Luke blindly, then her sight cleared and their eyes met and Judith felt her heart jump inside her, a physical sensation which left her breathless and shaken. Her skin began to burn and her mouth went dry.

My God, what's wrong with me? she thought. I'm not falling in love with him, am I? That would be crazy. I'd have to be a suitable case for psychiatric treatment if I let myself get infatuated with someone like Luke Doulton. No one had ever had that sort of effect on her before, she'd decided long ago that she wasn't the type who lost her head over a man, she had seen other girls trapped in an infatuation with someone they should have run from on first sight, and felt sorry for them; told herself that she had too much common sense. Her cherished common sense seemed to have deserted her now. Her heart kept taking queer little sideways leaps every time Luke smiled at her.

He was talking about work again and Judith pulled herself together. It was probably indigestion, she told herself firmly. That was all it was—indigestion. She must have eaten her lunch too fast.

CHAPTER SIX

DURING the days that followed Judith tried to convince herself that that flash of insight had been pure imagination. She kept a close watch on her feelings, monitoring them like a severe teacher ready to slap a pupil down the minute she showed signs of wandering attention. When Luke came into her office and she felt her nerves leap with fire she told herself it was irritation because he had broken her concentration, when he turned suddenly and smiled at her and she felt an unusual heat in her face she insisted on believing that it was pure embarrassment in case he so much as guessed what stupid ideas had been passing through her head. Not that she was quite sure how he would react if he did ever catch on—but she certainly wasn't going to risk it in any event. He might be amused, he might be embarrassed, either prospect appalled her.

From the first day they worked well together, though, that was a plus factor. It soon became obvious that they thought alike in many ways. Not only did she understand what Luke was planning before he so much as mentioned the subject, but she could anticipate where he would turn next and have the relevant papers easily to hand when he asked for them. She picked up little clues from things he said, background material he was looking at, but often it was simply that she knew instinctively what he was likely to do because in his place she would move in that direction. All the same, she had a lot to learn, and it helped to keep busy; she couldn't think much about Luke if she was racing through a pile of folders, trying to make sense of what they contained.

Doulton-Klein International was a complex web of interests stretching across the world. It took Judith most of that first week to discover exactly how far Luke's organisation stretched. Each evening she took home with her a vast pile of folders and worked on them after her evening meal. When Robert rang she had to excuse herself from meeting him for a while.

'I'd really love to see that film, but I'm up to my ears in work. Can I take a rain check?'

'All work and no play,' Robert said mildly.

'I know, and I'm sure it won't be long before I'm abreast of the job, but until then I've got to scramble to keep up with the day's meetings. I can't go in to talk to directors when I don't know what the hell they're burbling about, can I?'

'You sound irritable,' he commented.

'Sorry, just tired, it will wear off.'

'What about this weekend? Can't you take Saturday night off?'

'Saturday would be just fine, thanks.'

'I'll pick you up,' he offered, and she accepted gratefully. She went back to her paperwork feeling rather weary. Her eyes were beginning to blur from studying small print for hours and her brains were taking longer to assimilate the details of the papers she was reading. It was a rainy Thursday evening, she could hear the melancholy dripping of the eaves outside and the passing traffic swished on the wet roads, there was something vaguely depressing about everything, even her supper had tasted flavourless and dull.

Baba wasn't back from California yet. Judith had talked to Ruth on the phone the evening before; she had wanted to find out when Baba was returning, the sooner she was back and in visible possession of Luke the better Judith would feel.

'No, I haven't heard,' Ruth had said, however. 'Not so much as a postcard, but that doesn't surprise me. Baba never sends postcards. If she has any definite news she'll probably ring me.'

'If she gets the part, you mean?' Judith agreed with a sigh. She didn't wish Baba any harm, but she hoped she wouldn't get that part, otherwise she might be over there in California for months, and Judith wanted her back here with Luke. Having Baba around as a visible reminder that Luke belonged to her would make it easier to kill those stupid, senseless feelings which she was telling herself did not exist.

'Wouldn't it be wonderful if she did?' Ruth was excited at the very idea. 'You know, I've always felt certain that Baba was someone special.'

'What about Luke Doulton, though? Baba says he isn't going to like it.'

'I'm sure he'll be as proud as a peacock—after all, she'd be famous and if he loves her he'll be delighted for her.' It seemed so simple to Ruth, she projected her own attitudes on to other people and couldn't imagine that anyone might see things differently. Ruth was generous enough to be overjoyed by the possibility that her sister might become a famous film star; it didn't enter her head that Luke saw life from a different angle.

'Let me know if she gets the part, won't you?' said Judith, and Ruth laughed.

'You can bet I will, I'll be on the phone so fast I'll probably be incoherent!' She paused and asked; 'How's the job? Getting on okay with Luke? Is he difficult to work for?'

'We haven't actually come to blows yet,' Judith hedged, and a moment later rang off; she didn't want to say too much about Luke, you never knew what you were giving away when you talked to someone.

She put down her paperwork and went to the window, pulling back the curtain to watch the rain streaking down the glass. It matched her mood. She had often wondered what effect love really had on people; watching lovers from the outside one was often thrown back on the idea that it was all illusion, people looked for something outside themselves which might make their lives more bearable and they thought they had found it in another human being when all they had found was someone else to feel lonely with. Judith hadn't been able to imagine herself going crazy over another human being; she had thought herself too cool-headed, too independent, she had told herself that she would never make the mistake of believing that someone else could change the whole world for you. Now she was beginning to find out what havoc love could wreak—and she was confused, disorientated, bewildered.

The more she told herself not to look at him so much the more her eyes wandered in his direction. She had stored up a million tiny pictures of him now: Luke standing at a window, looking out, as she was doing now. Luke talking as he walked around her office, his hands in his pockets; his dark brown hair almost brushing his collar as he bent forward to look at a letter she showed him; the quick, sideways flicker of his eyes if they passed in the corridor; the secret smile with which he silently commented to her on something said in a board meeting, the shape and texture of his hand as he held a door open for her—she felt she was memorising him, imprinting him on her brain patterns. When he came into the building one morning while she was waiting for the lift she didn't have to turn to check that it was him: her body had antennae which registered his presence anywhere, the sound of his footsteps on the marble floor was unmistakable.

The phone rang and she jumped, letting the curtain drop. While she was moving across the room she pulled herself together; really, her nerves were right out of control. She had to do something about it, and soon.

'Hallo?'

'Judith?' Luke sounded brisk, in a hurry.

Her heart jumped. 'Yes,' she said, trying to sound cool.

'I'm afraid I won't be able to be at the board meeting tomorrow. Sir Isaac Kalsterg is flying in first thing in the morning and he wants to talk to me. You'll have to sit in for me. Could you come round here for a quick briefing? I've got all the documents here.'

She swallowed, her lips dry. 'Yes, when?'

'Now,' he said, sounding surprised. 'Sorry to drag you out on a night like this—I'd come over there, but I'm expecting some urgent calls, I can't go out. It won't take long.' A smile entered his voice. 'You're always very quick to pick things up.'

'Thanks,' she said, her mouth compressing. 'I'll be there in a quarter of an hour.'

'See you,' he said, and rang off. Judith replaced her own phone slowly, her hand trembling, and stood there for a minute frowning at nothing, then hurried into the bedroom to get ready. She didn't have time to change; if Luke objected to her arriving in old jeans and a blue shirt that was his problem. She ran a comb through her hair, renewed her make-up and slipped on a short beige raincoat. Looking at herself in the mirror helped to restore her sense of perspective—the very ordinary girl looking back at her was no threat to Baba's happiness. Luke wasn't going to look twice at her. All the insanity was on her side; she almost convinced herself she felt sorry for the poor man. It

must be a bore having women lose their heads over you,
and she could be sure she wasn't the first. Look at the way
Caroline Rendell had behaved at his engagement party!
Luke had been tight-lipped with rage, and who could
blame him? Whatever sort of relationship he had had with
Caroline she had behaved appallingly; she must have been
beside herself because he had rejected her in favour of
Baba, and Judith felt a painful fellow feeling for Caroline
now that she was so personally involved. It seemed ironic
that she should have snarled at Luke because she saw him
with Caroline at the nightclub that night only to go
slightly crazy over him herself later.

She left the flat and drove away with rain washing
down her windscreen and the wipers clacking uselessly
back and forth, barely clearing the glass long enough
for her to see the rear lights of the car in front of her.
The streets were almost deserted; sensible people were
not going out in this downpour, why hadn't she told
Luke that she was already in bed asleep when he rang?
Because you didn't think of it, you dummy, she told
herself, slowing even further as she skidded around a
corner on three wheels.

Luke lived in a palatial Nash house in a circular
terrace in Regents Park. Judith had to drive past it to
find a parking space and then run back with bent head
and rapidly saturated clothes to the gate. She dived
under the portico and rang the bell, shivering.

The door was opened by Luke in a cream and blue
diamond-patterned sweater and cream pants. He looked
at her with compunction. 'My God, you're wet! The
rain must have got worse.'

'Can I drip inside? It's cold out here,' said Judith
through her chattering teeth. He moved back and she
scuttled inside. Luke removed her wet coat and she
looked down at the damp mark she had left on his
carpet. She didn't apologise; served him right.

'There's a bathroom on the left at the end of the hall, you'd better dry your hair,' Luke told her. 'I'm sorry to have dragged you out in this weather; I didn't realise how hard it was raining. Would you like some hot milk or coffee? Or a glass of whisky or brandy?'

'Coffee would be fine, thanks,' said Judith, following him down the hall. Her feet sank into the deep pile of the pastel blue carpet, she looked back and saw her tracks following them like the muddy pawprints of a dog. Luke glanced back too and laughed.

'Never mind them—one of the servants will deal with them in the morning.'

Judith gave him a dry smile; wasn't he lucky, then? She went into the bathroom he indicated and rubbed her lank hair vigorously; it looked even worse than usual afterwards. She combed it, but it still looked hung round her face like string. She took off her shoes and placed them near the radiator; they might dry out in half an hour.

As she left the bathroom in her damp jeans and bare feet Luke emerged from another door carrying a tray of coffee and two cups and saucers. Judith's brows rose and he looked quickly at her expression. 'Now what?' he asked warily.

'Did you make the coffee yourself?'

'Why shouldn't I? I make very good coffee.'

'What happened to all the servants? Don't tell me they're on strike.'

'Unless I'm expecting visitors I always give them the evening off—there's no point in them hanging around in the kitchen with nothing to do. I think they're probably still watching a war film on TV. They live upstairs.' He waved a hand vaguely. 'The top floor.'

'How many are there?'

'Full-time? Only two—a married couple. Joe's my chauffeur and his wife runs the house; she has several part-time women helpers, there's a lot to do.' He pushed open another door, balancing the tray on his hip, and Judith followed him into a comfortable sitting-room. Luke put the tray down while she was looking around her at the smooth, ivory walls and pale green carpet, the rectangular couches facing each other with a squared black table between them, the floor-length olive green curtains shutting out the rainy night. An enormous landscape painting hung on one wall: a shadowy oil-painting of some age whose high elms and green hills led the eye further and further into it to be lost in a misty perspective. Judith glanced at the other objects in the room, quickly noting a bronze urn, a noble and rather forbidding stone head, a lacquered cabinet of black and gold and several bowls of spring flowers whose scent was faint and poignant. On the table was laid out a chess game; beside it a pile of folders and a book open face down on the wood.

Luke looked over his shoulder at her: 'Come to the fire. Cream and sugar in your coffee?'

'No, black; no sugar, thanks.' Judith knelt by the fire, holding her hands to it. She was rather surprised to see it; it was years since she had sat by a fire, in New York everything was centrally heated.

Luke moved, handed her the coffee. 'Here you are.'

His fingers touched her own; she kept her eyes down. 'Thank you.' To distract herself from his proximity she asked: 'Do you play chess with yourself?'

'When there's nobody else available. I play master games from books, trying to think out a way of beating the other man.' He sat down in a corner of one of the couches, nursing his cup. 'Do you play?'

'A little.'

'I thought you might.'

She looked at him, hearing the dry note in his voice,

and he smiled at her. 'Anyone with a mind like yours would have to be a good chess player.'

'I didn't say I was good,' she pointed out.

'You didn't have to. I've seen you working on a problem; I'm sure you're a very formidable chess player.'

She curled round on the carpet, sipping her coffee with the fire heating one side of her face. It provided an excuse for the flush she could feel. 'I'd better hear what I'm to say at the board meeting tomorrow,' she reminded him, and he nodded, one hand tapping the folders on the table.

'I've got all the details in here, but I'd better run through it with you.' He began to talk and she listened, drinking her coffee. On the table a small lyre clock chimed musically; Judith looked at it in surprise. Half past ten. She had been here for half an hour; the time had flown. Luke looked at the clock too.

'It's getting late. I think I've given you the gist of my views, anyway. If you run into any real trouble shelve it and I'll talk to them later, but I doubt if there'll be any problems. I'm sure I can trust you to deal with it.'

She tried not to smile; it was stupid to be so delighted by his compliment, but she couldn't help it.

Luke rose, but before she could get up too he was beside her, touching her hair lightly with one hand. She stiffened.

'It's dry now,' he said. 'You looked as if you'd just been pulled out of a river when you arrived.' He was still stroking her hair and she pulled her head back without being too obvious about it, getting up at the same time. She shot him a wary look and found him staring at her; a strange expression in his grey eyes, she wasn't sure what to call it. Hesitation, uncertainty, surprise ... Judith looked away before she could be sure.

'Do you still see Robert Gordon?' Luke asked.

'Yes, frequently, why?' Her mind was still half running on business; she did not expect his reply when it came.

'Are you in love with him?'

'What?' Judith's head lifted and she stared at him, open-mouthed. A slow flush crawled up her face. 'That's a very personal question; if I was it would be no affair of yours.'

He didn't argue the point. He asked instead in the same thoughtful, considering tone: 'Have you *ever* been in love?'

Judith fizzed with annoyance. 'The same answer applies—what is this? Why the interest in my private life?'

'Just curious,' he shrugged, looking oddly confused, as though he wasn't sure, himself, why he was quizzing her about her love life. 'You're so calm and self-contained; I just wondered about you. Don't you ever get curious about other people's feelings and thoughts? It's easy when they're open about them; but people like you are like locked safes. I just wondered if there was a combination that would open you up.'

'Do your safe-cracking elsewhere,' said Judith, moving with purpose towards the door.

'Are you going?' he asked, sounding surprised. 'Don't be so touchy. Is Gordon such a sensitive subject? I hope he isn't trying to poach you for his firm.'

'He offered me a job ages ago,' she told him with satisfaction.

He smiled. 'But you refused.'

He was too quick. 'The job's still open if I ever change my mind,' she told him tartly.

He considered her wryly, then bent and picked up the folders they had been discussing. 'Don't forget these—you'll want them.'

She came back and took them from him, but when she had them in her grasp Luke's fingers took hold of her wrists and held her firmly. She looked up, startled. 'I wouldn't want to lose you now; if you ever have any problems in the firm, talk to me, don't even think of going elsewhere.'

She looked up at him, her lips parted, trembling. Luke's fingers tightened, he began to pull her towards him and she felt her throat beating with a heady pulse. Her eyes widened, darkened, focusing on his mouth, following the warm hard curve of it with a sensual awareness which ached inside her.

'Promise to do that?' Luke asked in a low, husky voice.

Judith nodded, knowing that he was looking fixedly at her. The room was suddenly so quiet that she heard every tiny sound in it with a leap of the nerves: the rain beating against the windows, the tick of the clocks, the muted flare of a flame shooting out of the fire. She knew that if she took one small step their mouths would meet; she knew he was looking at her in exactly the same way that she was looking at him, every nerve in her body was conscious of his stare.

'I'd better go,' she muttered, pulling away with an effort of will power. He was dangerous; a hypnotist whose stare could beat down all your efforts to escape. She wanted to feel his mouth on her own with a hunger that hurt, but she reminded herself of Baba, she told herself how despicable it was of her to think like this, how contemptuous she had been when she saw him with Caroline Rendell. Now here she was, dying to put he own arms round his neck and kiss him on that beautiful warm mouth. She was furious with herself; what did she think she was doing? How many warnings did she need before she saw the folly of allowing herself to feel like that about this man?

He let go of her wrists, she bolted to the door and found her dry shoes in the bathroom, trod into them hurriedly and walked to the front door with Luke in silence. He opened the door and the rain beat down on the white stone steps.

'I'd better make a dash for it,' said Judith with relief, diving out into the night. She ran to her parked car, aware that the front door still stood open; a yellow shaft of light splashed across the wet pavements and Luke was watching her from under the portico. When she drove away, though, he had gone back into the house and shut the door.

It was very hard to get to sleep that evening; Judith kept reliving the moments in the quiet room when she had so nearly let Luke kiss her—or she had so nearly kissed him. She wasn't sure what would have happened. Looking back, she wasn't even sure she hadn't imagined the whole thing, her mind was no longer the cool, careful piece of apparatus on which she had relied during her whole career. It was behaving in an unpredictable and worrying way; if she relaxed and forgot to watch her mind it slipped the leash and came bounding back to her with images of Luke that kept her awake into the small hours.

Be sensible, she told herself scoldingly. Why should he have wanted to kiss you? Look at yourself, for heaven's sake. He's engaged to Baba. She's ravishing; magazines pay a fortune to have her face on their covers. Why would any sane man who was engaged to her want to flirt with you? A reflex action, maybe, a token pass just because he always makes passes at a woman if he's alone with her ... but no, she no longer believed that that was what Luke was like. He simply didn't behave like that; at least she had never seen him doing so. Charming and amusing, he certainly was, but he was also very intelligent, very shrewd and a formidable man to work for or with. The two sides of his nature would not add up and therefore one of them must be wrong. His reputation as a womaniser obviously had some basis in fact, though. What about the pretty redhead he had been with at the 21 Club?

Judith's face burned as he remembered the way he had looked her over that day and then walked away when John began to introduce her. Luke hadn't thought she was worth meeting. Did he remember seeing her before? she wondered, and doubted it.

She went into work next day with a splitting headache and had to go through the very tedious board meeting in a state of permanent nausea. She staggered into her own office later and sat down, her head on the desk, pressing her cupped hands into her eyes, to relieve the ache behind them.

'What's wrong?' a voice said close at hand, and she lifted her head, eyes half shut, to look at Luke.

'Migraine,' she said, and it hurt to speak, there were flashing lights in front of her eyes; the zigzag semi-circles which always came with migraine.

'You'd better go home. I get them myself; I've got some pills which help.' Luke put a hand under her elbow and lifted her. She was almost unaware of going down in the lift, getting into his car. The chauffeur was running towards them across the concrete; his feet seemed to crash inside her head and she winced, but in the underground car park it was very dark and soothing. She leaned her head back against the upholstery and let her lids droop. The car began to move smoothly up the ramp.

Luke came into her flat with her and made her lie down on the couch. He vanished and returned with a glass of water and two pink torpedo-shaped pills.

'Take these.'

Judith took them, drank the water, murmured drily:

'Thanks,' and lay back again. Luke put a quilt over her and drew the curtains. She sighed with relief in the darkness.

'I'm going back to the office. Don't worry about work, just try to sleep. If you aren't well tomorrow, don't come in . . .' he murmured.

She whispered: 'Thank you.' It was hard to speak; impossible to think.

Luke sat down on the edge of the couch and brushed her tumbled hair back from her hot face with a gentle hand. Judith kept her eyes shut. 'Sorry about this,' she managed to get out, and Luke bent over her, his mouth lightly brushed against hers and then was gone again. A moment later so was he; she heard the door close quietly and tears squeezed out from under her lids. Her face was still wet as she went to sleep.

She woke up in the dark and couldn't remember where she was for a minute, then she swung off the couch and put on the light. It was nine o'clock at night and she had slept for hours; it must have been nearly two by the time Luke left her. Seven solid hours of sleep, she thought, disgusted with her own weakness. She went into the bathroom, feeling dishevelled and hot, and had a refreshing shower, then slipped into a long white towelling robe and went into the kitchen. She was parched and dry; she needed some tea.

She was sitting in front of the television, drinking the tea, when the phone went. She tripped over the hem of her robe as she rushed to answer it.

'Judith? Is that you?'

'Baba? Yes, of course it's me—where are you?'

'In my flat, I'm back in London.'

'How was the audition?' Judith couldn't make out whether Baba was over the moon or depressed; her voice wasn't giving any clues and Judith didn't like to ask bluntly: did you get the part?

'Nerve-racking, and I still don't know if I've got a chance or not. They're very cagey; they said they'll be in touch.'

'At least they didn't say you hadn't got it; there's still a chance.'

'My agent says they'll probably have me back to do some more tests if they like the first one. I had to come home to do a job in London tomorrow, but I'll be going back after that. My agent says it's important for me to be available if they ask for me.' Baba laughed and Judith heard the optimism in her voice then; she was half relieved that Baba had reappeared and half regretful because she wasn't staying. It would be much easier to fight her own feeling of attraction towards Luke if Baba was there to remind her that he belonged to someone else.

As coolly as she could, Judith asked: 'Have you seen Luke yet?'

'He was busy when I rang. I only got here two hours ago; I feel half dead after that flight from Los Angeles. It seems like a hundred years ago since I set out. Luke's secretary said she'd try to get a message to him, but he's dining with some politician and he won't be able to get away before midnight, she thinks. Judith, can I come and have a drink? I'm bored, I feel so restless. I didn't want to come back; I'm afraid that I'll miss my chance if I'm not there on the spot, but my agent said I couldn't get out of the job tomorrow. I can't sit around here alone, I've got to talk to someone.'

'Be my guest,' said Judith with wry amusement. She did not want to see Baba, but she could hardly say so. Baba had a sort of cheerful disregard for what anyone else wanted; why hadn't that struck her before? Looking back, that was how it had always been. Baba always went for what she wanted and if you were in her way she very sweetly walked right over you, apologising as she did so. In anybody else it would be a horrible trait, but Baba was so nice; she made you feel she was doing you a favour by running your life to suit herself. How could you be so niggardly as to resent it?

She rang off, tidied the sitting-room, made some fresh coffee and brushed her drying hair into some semblance of order by the time Baba arrived.

'Hallo, darling; you're so sweet to put up with me. I brought you something from California,' Baba said when she opened the door to her, putting a parcel into her hands.

'Oh, thank you,' Judith said, following her into the sitting-room and opening the gaily wrapped box. It was a bracelet of small green stones, polished and unevenly shaped; the sort of souvenir tourists find everywhere. 'How lovely,' said Judith, smoothing the stones with one fingertip. 'How nice of you to think of me.'

'I'm dying for some coffee,' said Baba, sitting down and pouring herself a cup. 'I got several of those bracelets for people; I wasn't sure what to bring back, but that sort of thing does for anyone.'

'Yes,' Judith said, dropping the bracelet back into its box.

'How are you getting on with Luke? You haven't told him about my screen test, have you?' Baba gave her a vivid smile, quite certain that she hadn't but reminding her of her promise. 'I've rung him every night to tell him how much I've missed him. I could tell he didn't know.'

Judith poured herself some coffee; she was in that halcyon state which follows migraine when you feel very calm and clear and nothing bothers you.

'It felt funny when I got off the plane at Heathrow and saw so many pale people; everyone in California is so suntanned. On the beach you see such gorgeous-looking men; Americans are so keen on keeping fit and getting brown. Luke spends too much time in the office, I'll have to coax him out into the fresh air. We could have such a good time over there, and after all, he's American; most of his business is over there, but he lives in New York or Vermont and the weather isn't half so good there. I like to get down on the beach.'

'With all the gorgeous men?' Judith enquired, and got a wicked look in response to that.

Baba laughed. 'Don't be naughty—that's not what I meant at all, although if you saw them, Judith ... rippling muscles and lovely golden skin ... fantastic! If I get this part I'll have to spend a lot of time there, anyway. Everyone lives in California.'

'Everyone?' Judith queried drily.

'Who matters,' Baba expanded. 'There's no reason why Luke shouldn't spend half the year there; it's no further from New York than London.'

'Have you suggested it yet?'

Baba looked at her pityingly. 'Of course not; I haven't mentioned it. If I don't get this part there wouldn't be any point.'

'No, of course, silly of me.' Judith looked at her soberly. 'Baba, if you don't get the part what will you do?'

Baba shrugged. 'Have a baby, I expect—that's what Luke wants, and if I'm not going into films I might as well give up modelling and start a family right away. Of course, I'd like children later on if I do get the part, but I'd have to put it off for a year or two.' She poured herself some more coffee; under the pure silk dress her curved body moved with tigerish grace, Judith could see exactly how she would come over on celluloid, it would be a pity if she missed the chance, and she said so impulsively.

'Oh, darling, do you really think so?' Baba was neon-lit with delight. 'I'll die, you know, absolutely die if I don't get this part!'

'I doubt it, Baba,' Judith said gently.

'Well, of course, *you* wouldn't understand ...' Baba said impatiently. 'I *know* this is for me.' She slid a hand under her blonde curls, lifting them in a restless gesture, her body arched in yearning like a woman aching for a lover. 'I know it is!'

'Well, I hope you get what you want,' said Judith, watching her.

'Ruth thinks I'm crazy,' Baba confided suddenly. 'She doesn't understand, either. She'd always choose a man rather than a career; you're not that stupid. Aren't I right, Judith? I mean, I'm no rabid feminist, I adore men, personally, I couldn't live without them, but I'd stifle if I had to live like Ruth. David's a sweetie and I'm very fond of him, but it would be ghastly to be stuck in a house all day with housework and shopping and kids.' She was very earnest now, leaning forward on the couch, her beautiful face alight as she talked and the vivid yellow shimmer of her silk dress reflecting the lamp light.

'It depends what you want out of life,' conceded Judith. She couldn't fault Baba's reasoning; if a career was what she really wanted who had the right to criticise her? 'But what about Luke?' She had to force his name out, she hoped her voice and face did not betray anything to Baba.

Baba made an anguished face; she did it beautifully, and if Judith hadn't know her so well she would have suspected that Baba was acting, but then Baba was always very conscious of herself whatever she did, she couldn't even pour a cup of coffee without doing it to perfection and with one eye on her audience.

'I *know* ... I'm torn, honestly, Judith, utterly distraught every time I try to make up my mind to tell him I want to go into films. It will be such a terrible shock to him, I'd die rather than break his heart, I'm quite crazy about him; if he didn't have a penny to his name I'd still want to marry him. His money makes no difference to me, it's Luke who turns me on—but does being in love mean you have to stop doing everything else? I mean, he isn't going to give up his career for me, is he? Can you imagine it? It's so funny, the very idea ...' She laughed, her head back and her curls tumbling around her amused face in wanton profusion. She really ought to be in films, Judith thought; she's a natural for them.

The door bell rang brusquely and Judith jumped. 'Who on earth can that be at this hour?' She looked at the clock. It was gone eleven.

'Oh, that will be Luke—I left a message for him to pick me up here. I came by taxi, but you can never be sure of getting one back and I didn't want to drag you out in the middle of the night unless I had to.'

'How thoughtful of you,' said Judith, wishing she hadn't asked Luke to come here. She watched Baba rush to the door and then turned and collected up the coffee things, clattering the cups to avoid overhearing their first embrace. It didn't quite work; her ears were hyper-sensitive tonight, and Baba didn't hurry her kisses.

'Darling, darling, oh, I've missed you ... mmm ... do that again ...'

Judith wished she had shut the door before she went out. She half turned her head angrily and saw Baba curving her body against Luke, her arms round his neck and her face raised to his. She had her eyes closed and her lips parted. Luke looked at Judith over her head and moved Baba away with both hands on her shoulders.

'Say goodnight to Judith and we'll be on our way.'

'Don't be rude, Luke,' protested Baba, a pout altering the invitation on her mouth. 'Come and say hello to poor Judith; just because she's one of your serfs there's no reason to treat her like one!'

Judith slammed the sugar bowl on to the silver tray and Baba pulled a reluctant Luke into the room behind her.

'We were just having coffee—is there any left, Judith? Oh, you've started to clear it away—well, never mind. You're so efficient, Judith—I do admire you for that. I'm hopeless about housework and stuff.'

'You're unlikely to have to do any,' Judith said drily, lifting the tray.

Luke took it from her. He walked towards the kitchen and Baba picked up her delicate white high-heeled sandals, which she had kicked off earlier, and sat down to put them on. Luke reappeared and asked Judith quietly: 'How's the head?'

'Fine, thank you. Those pills worked wonderfully.'

'Good,' he said, looking away.

'Have you given poor Judith a headache, you slave-driver?' Baba asked, looking up as she slid the strap through the buckle of her shoe. 'How wicked of you, you mustn't be cruel to Judith, she's my *oldest* friend.'

'Thank you,' said Judith, feeling older than anyone else in the world. 'I get migraine from time to time, that's all. It had nothing to do with work.'

'Yes, it did,' Luke said brusquely. 'You've been working too hard. I shouldn't have pushed you.'

'You didn't push, you didn't need to—I work at my own pace.'

'All the same, slow down. You looked quite ill today. I was worried.'

'Oh, isn't he sweet?' smiled Baba, standing up. 'You get a kiss for that; wasn't it clever of me to find Judith for you?'

'Very clever,' Luke agreed, and as she stood on tiptoe

to kiss him said with a tired smile: 'Baba, it is gone eleven—we ought to be on our way.'

She persisted in giving him a kiss, then said: 'I must go to the loo—I won't be a second, darling, don't get into a tizz. Judith, haven't you got a whisky or something to give the brute?' She drifted out without waiting to get an answer.

'I've got some whisky,' Judith said without looking at him.

'I've already had quite enough to drink for one evening. I've been dining with one of the biggest bores in Westminster; drink was the only refuge to hand.'

She laughed spontaneously at his wry voice; their eyes met and she almost jumped at the expression in his. Her mouth moved without uttering a sound, forming the word: 'Don't.' She wasn't even aware of doing it, the word was ringing in her head like bells under water. Don't look at me like that, you mustn't!

He looked so tired, she thought. His eyes moved away from her suddenly, as though he had detached them with difficulty. 'Your flat's so quiet. I had a hell of an evening. I wondered how you were; I couldn't stop yawning while that fool was mumbling on at me. I'd have given anything to be playing chess with . . .' He stopped, his voice raw, and Judith went hot and then icy cold.

'With one of your chess master opponents back in your flat,' she supplied in as level a voice as she could manage.

He smiled wryly. 'Of course.' A pause, then he asked: 'Did you sleep?'

'For seven hours.'

'My God, you must have been tired! You shouldn't let yourself get into that sort of state.'

'We can't always help ourselves,' Judith said flatly, and Luke looked back at her with a grim, intent expression.

'No.'

Baba came back; she had managed to do the impossible—make herself look even more beautiful. She wound her hand through Luke's arm, her hair decorating his dark sleeve. He looked, Judith thought miserably, quite unbearably good-looking in his evening suit and stiff white shirt; a perfect foil for Baba's blonde beauty. Baba knew it, too. She smiled at Judith happily, her mouth pink and glossy.

'Darling, you're so good to me. It's been a lovely evening.' She glanced sideways at Luke, her blue eyes teasing. 'Luke would much prefer me to spend an evening with you than with some gorgeous man, wouldn't you, Luke?'

'Much,' said Luke, and Baba laughed.

'We must have another party soon, a cosy little one— you and me, darling, and we'll find a man for Judith.'

Judith was rigid with outrage, but before she could snap angrily Luke steered Baba out of the room; almost hustling her along with an arm around her back. 'Goodnight,' he said shortly as he yanked Baba through the front door.

'Goodnight,' Judith said, closing it on the pair of them and forcibly restraining herself from slamming it. She walked back into the sitting-room and picked up one of the sofa cushions which Baba had been leaning on; it bore the soft imprint of her warm body. Judith punched it back into shape and threw it down again, then she went and did the washing up with brisk energy. Find a man for Judith . . . what a nerve! Baba never thought before she opened her mouth. She had no idea that she was being insulting; Judith was sure of that. Baba wouldn't dream of being spiteful, she simply didn't realise how what she said could sting. Find a man for Judith . . . as though they might have to scour the four corners of the world to find anyone willing to put up with her for a whole evening. Baba didn't think she could get a man; that was the point. She had rung here this evening, sure of finding Judith in; it wouldn't have entered her head that Judith might be out on a date, that she wouldn't always be sitting here ready to provide a listening ear for Baba's problems.

Judith went to bed in a mood of angry irritation. She couldn't get to sleep again; she kept imagining Baba and Luke in his house, in his bed. Where else would they have gone at this hour? Jealousy burned her like swallowed acid; she turned over and punched her pillow, furious with herself.

He had been odd tonight; quiet and withdrawn; what had he been thinking when he looked at her in that grim way? His mood had seemed to be a reflection of her own, but that was just wishful thinking, pure imagination. Whatever had been wrong with Luke had nothing to do with her.

CHAPTER SEVEN

SHE met Luke as she got out of the lift next morning. He looked at her, his eyes penetrating. 'You still look pale—didn't you sleep last night?'

'Yes, thank you,' she said coldly. Some demon made her ask him: 'Did you?' Or had he been awake half the night, making love to Baba?

'Yes, I was exhausted after my four hours of tedium with that old fool Wentlow. I dropped Baba at her flat and went home and straight to bed. I slept like a log.'

'Oh,' said Judith, suddenly lighthearted. 'Good.'

'She's flying to the States again tomorrow, she tells me, but I can't see her tonight, I've got to fly to Sydney this afternoon. I'll be away for a few days. You can manage while I'm gone, can't you? I'll keep in touch on the phone, but I'd be glad if you'd ring my mother every day, and tell her what's been happening.'

'Of course,' Judith said, wondering if that was to please his mother or to keep a check on her.

She was kept very busy all day and was still hard at work when Luke came into her office that afternoon, his Burberry over his arm.

'I'm just off. Don't work too hard while I'm away.' His eyes held a wry intimacy. 'I don't want to hear you've been having any more migraines—especially as I won't be here to deal with them!'

Judith tried to smile and couldn't. Luke stood there, watching her, his grey eyes full of a feeling she couldn't miss but dared not admit she noticed.

'Well, have a good flight,' she said huskily.

'Thank you,' he said, his mouth twisting, then he

turned and walked out, and she stared at where he had been with eyes that had blurred. Eye strain again, she told herself; she must see an optician if this went on.

While Luke was in Australia, he rang Judith, every day; his voice coming and going in a buzz of crackle so that she lost the odd word. 'Yes, everything's fine here,' she would yell, and he would say in dry amusement, 'No need to shout, I can hear you as if we were in the same room.' And then she would turn her head in superstitious uneasiness half expecting to see him behind her. She got to know when he was smiling from the sound of his voice; when she rang off she would sit staring at the phone and seeing his grey eyes with that smile in them. 'My mother says you keep in touch every day,' he said once. 'Thank you for taking the trouble, I know you're up to your ears at the moment.'

'I'm going down to see her on Sunday,' Judith told him.

'Good, give her my love.'

'I will,' she said, hoping her voice didn't sound husky. If she ever had Luke's love, she thought, the last thing she would do was give it to anybody. 'When are you getting back?'

'Monday, if I'm lucky, I'll have to see how things go.' She looked at the calendar on her desk and counted the days like a child waiting for Christmas. When she had put the phone down she had to force her mind back to work, but it wasn't easy.

She had her grandmother to dinner on Saturday night. Robert was the other guest and helped Judith in the kitchen before Mrs Murry arrived. He opened the door wearing an apron and Mrs Murry was quite shocked. 'Poor Robert, you shouldn't make him work for his dinner,' she scolded Judith. Mrs Murry had never once asked her husband to peel carrots or make a salad dressing. 'Our generation didn't,' she said. 'I wouldn't have wanted him in the kitchen, anyway, that was my province. If men get into the kitchen, there'll be nowhere private to go, you know.' Judith listened, smiling; she didn't argue, but her grandmother knew very well she did not agree.

Robert chimed in: 'I've had a whale of a time, Mrs Murry—cooking is fun. Who do you think cooks my meals? I'm a pretty good cook, although I say it myself.'

'You need a wife,' Mrs Murry told him firmly, and Judith moved away, her face impatient.

'Now why didn't that occur to me?' said Robert, laughing. 'You're very bright, Mrs Murry, that's what I need, all right—a slave to do all my domestic work for me.'

'Don't look at me,' Judith said over her shoulder, then wished she hadn't said it.

'Is that a proposal? I accept,' Robert said with amusement, and her grandmother looked from one to the other of them, obviously wondering how serious the discussion was meant to be.

'Forget it,' Judith teased, laughing. She did not want her grandmother to get the wrong idea, nor did she want Robert to think the wrong things, either. 'At least I get paid for my slavery at work. Unpaid slave is a job I'm not applying for.'

'Feminist!' Robert jeered, and she bowed.

'Thank you.' She pointed to the sink. 'For that you can do the washing up.'

When she was alone again that night the flat seemed oddly empty and silent; she lay listening to the sound of traffic, the noise of people walking along the road outside, and felt lonely. There was a queer, persistent ache inside her. She switched on the radio and a female singer with a sob in her voice began to moan out her longing. Judith angrily switched off again—the woman sounded like a cat on a moonlit night, sitting on a roof and wailing at the stars. Judith could do without that. She curled up in the warm bed trying to get to sleep, but the words of the plaintive love song sang inside her head; the lyric was hardly pure poetry, but the simple, poignant words kept on being repeated, they seemed to mean something, but she wasn't sure what, she only knew they got to her, they really got to her, and that made her angrier than ever.

For years she had kept calmly to the path she had laid out for herself, contented enough with her work, her friends, her well-organised days. Sometimes she had stopped to think: is this all? Sometimes she had felt a lack, an empty space somewhere inside her, she had been briefly nostalgic for something she had never had and could not even put a name to—but after that pause for thought in the midst of a lively day she had gone on enjoying what she was doing, whether it was casting an assessing eye over a company balance sheet or sitting in a theatre on Broadway watching a black comedy with someone who would take her on to supper afterwards. Those instants of personal doubt had never lasted, Judith had too much sense to dwell on them, she had instinctively felt that to do so would be to look down from a high wire. The probable result would be a fall, so she always coolly looked up again and went on unwaveringly.

What was happening to her now was much worse. She knew she was walking that high wire unsteadily, sinkingly aware of the abyss beneath. She knew what it was that she needed to fill the empty space inside her and she knew she could not have it. The feeling obsessing her was not so much frustration, although she certainly felt grimly conscious of the fact that what she wanted was out of reach and always would be—it was a seeping sadness because the one man she had ever felt like this about should be forbidden to her, and she knew it was a hundred to one against her ever finding anyone remotely like him.

She had waited years to fall in love and then done so with the wrong man. It seemed so unfair.

She was up very early next day to drive to Lambourne. On a fine Sunday morning in early summer the Kent countryside had a clarity and tenderness which made driving through it a permanent delight. Judith had trouble concentrating on the road ahead, she kept looking sideways at the landscape, her eyes dreamy. Love was undermining her, she thought impatiently; she felt her foundations crumbling. Six months ago she would have looked at the scenery, thought 'Hmm, pretty', then turned her attention back to what really mattered, whether the old blue van in front of her was really intending to move to the right at any second or whether the driver had forgotten to switch off his right side light which had been blinking for several miles now. You merely ran into trouble if, instead of giving your attention to the road ahead, you kept gazing romantically at the alluring prospects on either side, and that applied to life as well as to driving a car.

When she finally turned into the long drive and parked outside the house she found another car parked there. She walked to the front door, wondering if there were to be other guests for lunch. Mrs Doulton hadn't told her she was inviting anyone else, and Judith couldn't help feeling rather disappointed. She had been looking forward to talking about Luke to his mother, there were a thousand questions she wanted to ask about him, but she would have to be subtle about it, she couldn't just sit down like a reporter and fire off personal questions. His mother would wonder what on earth was going on! Judith had meant to angle their conversation with the hope of eliciting the answers she wanted without Mrs Doulton realising that she was being interrogated.

The front door opened abruptly, but it wasn't Fanny facing her, it was a small girl in a red swimsuit. Judith stared down at the round, clear-skinned face and long straight brown hair, and the child's hazel eyes stared back at her.

'Hallo,' Judith said uncertainly. 'I'm Judith.'

'Hallo, I know who you are. You're to go up to Grandma's bedroom, they left me here to wait for you 'cos Fanny's in the garden picking mint, but she'll be back in two shakes of a lamb's tail.' The little girl used the phrase unconsciously, but Judith could hear Fanny's grumpy voice behind it. 'We're swimming, they said I could come when you got here.' She grinned suddenly, showing small, irregular teeth. 'I can dive, can you dive? It's easy.' There was a light scattering of freckles across the bridge of her nose and her grin was mischievous. 'I'm going to creep up behind Daddy and push him in; that's what the boys do at school.'

'Make sure he's wearing his swimsuit first,' Judith told her, and the child laughed. She must be one of Angela's children; Pauline had said she only had one son, so the little girl could not belong to her. Judith liked Angela, she would enjoy meeting her again, but Pauline was far too sharp and critical; she had a censorious eye.

'See you,' the little girl said, disappearing at a run. Judith went into the house, her fingers crossed behind her back as she went up the stairs. Please, don't let Pauline be here, she pleaded with fate; that would ruin the day.

She tapped on Mrs Doulton's door and heard her call: 'Come in!'

'Hallo,' said Judith, smiling across the room, and

Mrs Doulton held out a hand. Judith went over to the bed and sat down.

'It's nice of you to give up one of your precious days off to me,' Mrs Doulton said, smiling at her.

'It's such a lovely day, I can't think of a nicer way of spending it,' Judith told her, and Mrs Doulton patted her hand.

'You're looking tired, have you been working too hard?'

'I've got a lot to learn in a very short time—this job is a million light years from the work I've been doing, there's so much more to it.'

'All the same, you mustn't push yourself too hard, it doesn't pay in the long run. My husband always said that if you work so hard that you're too tired to unwind after leaving the office you're heading for trouble.' Mrs Doulton leaned back, her eyes serious. 'I hope Luke isn't difficult to work for.'

'He's impossible to work for,' Judith said lightly, laughing, then shook her head. 'No, I think I already see the light at the end of the road, and Luke isn't a hard boss, he takes a lot of trouble to explain things clearly. I'm fascinated by the job.' She tried to keep her tone light, she hoped her smile looked natural—she remembered all too vividly that Mrs Doulton was not easily taken in by forced smiles. She had immediately seen through Caroline Rendell's smiles; Judith hoped her own eyes were not as betraying as Caroline's had been.

Hurriedly Judith changed the subject. 'Who was the little girl who opened the door?'

'Stephanie, my daughter Angela's eldest—she's been keeping me company.'

'She's about six, is she?'

Mrs Doulton nodded. 'Angela has a three-year-old, too; Benny. They're all down at the pool, I should have told you to bring a swimsuit. I'm sorry, I forgot; I think Angela has a spare if you'd like to . . .'

'Oh, no, it doesn't matter, I'd rather sit and talk to you. I wanted to ask you how Doulton-Klein International came into being—that was your husband's doing, I suppose? He set it up, didn't he?'

'In 1946,' Mrs Doulton said, her eyes moving to the window. The blue sky had that impossible radiance that an English summer has for far too brief a time; Mrs Doulton seemed to be watching the far distance, her eyes wide and nostalgic. She was looking back into the past. She talked about her husband, about the early days of their marriage, and Judith listened intently, realising that Mrs Doulton had almost forgotten she was there, she had no need to say anything because the older woman was half talking to herself, remembering aloud what she no doubt often remembered in silence.

Judith couldn't hear enough about Luke's background, hearing about his father and the rise of the organisation helped her to understand him better. Nobody springs from a void; everyone comes from somewhere and their past, their childhood and family, can explain their present, if you have the right clues. Judith felt a hungry curiosity about Luke, no detail was too small for her, she was busily filing it all away while she listened.

'He never told me how ill he was,' Mrs Doulton said some time later. 'When he died so suddenly the shock almost killed me. Luke was still so young, he had been working his way through the firm, learning all he could, but some of the board thought he wasn't ready to take over his father's position. There was a lot of backstairs intrigue and in-fighting; it was all very nasty, and I think it toughened Luke to have to face that out of the blue. Once I was sure he was past the worst, that he was safely in control, I bought this house and came over to

England. I thought it would be best; I was part of the past, Luke had to forge his own weapons. Of course he asked my advice and I was always ready to discuss the firm and advise him if I could, but he had to do it on his own in the last resort. It seemed best for him to start off the way he would have to go on ...' She looked at Judith wryly. 'It wasn't easy to step out of the picture. I'd spent most of my married life talking the business over with his father. I enjoyed being part of it all. But you have to know when to let go, and Luke had to be free.'

'He still values your advice, he told me so,' Judith told her gently.

Mrs Doulton laughed. 'I hope he goes, but I'm still very careful to wait to be asked for it. There's nothing worse than a mother who won't let go of her children; it must make it very hard for them to grow up.'

Fanny came into the room with some coffee and Judith solemnly said: 'Good morning, Fanny.'

'Morning,' said Fanny, handing her a cup of coffee. She looked at Mrs Doulton measuringly. 'You look tired, you should have a nap before lunch.' Her grim eyes went back to Judith. 'She has to rest for at least an hour morning and afternoon, you'd better take a walk in the garden when you've finished your coffee.'

When she had gone Mrs Doulton said ruefully: 'She's worked for me since I first got married, she's eight years older than I am and she never forgets it, I don't honestly know what I'd do if I lost Fanny, she's as much part of my life as Luke.' She smiled at Judith. 'Don't let her manner offend you; she doesn't mean to be rude.'

'I can see she's very fond of you, she's only trying to protect you,' Judith reassured her. 'She doesn't offend me.'

Ten minutes later she left Mrs Doulton and went downstairs and out into the sunny garden. The air was filled with the fragrance of newly mown grass and flowers. The day was very warm now that the sun had risen high in the sky, the mingled scent of early roses and lilac drifted to her nostrils as she followed the sound of voices through the garden.

The swimming pool was built just below the house with a belt of trees to shield it from view and keep the worst of the wind at bay. Judith emerged on the tiled pavement just as Stephanie launched herself into the water with a resounding splash.

'Not so violently, darling,' Angela complained in a languid voice. She was lying on a quilted lounger, her pregnancy barely concealed by the skirted swimsuit she wore. Hearing Judith's footsteps, she turned her head and waved a lazy hand.

'Hi, nice to see you.'

The others trod water to stare at Judith. Angela's husband, his hair slicked back wetly against his head, smiled at her and said: 'Hallo there.'

Angela took off the sunglasses she wore and gestured with them to the lounger beside her. 'Come and talk to me. Is Mother asleep?'

'Fanny told her she ought to be,' Judith said, and Angela laughed.

'She's a dragon, isn't she? I was scared stiff of her when I was little.'

Judith sat down, feeling a little out of place in her thin turquoise shift dress and sandals, when everyone else was in swimsuits.

'Is your sister here too?' Judith asked, and Angela shook her head.

'Pauline shot off back to civilisation, as she calls it. She loves it over in Geneva, she thinks England is boring.'

'Neither of you live in America; don't you get homesick?'

'I sometimes yearn for toasted marshmallows on top of hot chocolate,' Angela said. 'Gorgeous! But very fattening, so maybe I'm better off without it. We got over to Vermont for a fortnight in April; I do miss Vermont, we have a peaceful place there. Luke keeps it, but he doesn't often visit.'

They talked for a while, then Angela's little boy climbed dripping out of the pool and came over, shivering, demanding to be dried. 'I'm cold, I want to get dressed, Mummy.'

'I'll do it, shall I?' Judith offered as Angela began to hoist herself up with obvious reluctance. Picking up the enormous bath sheet, she wrapped Benny in its folds and began to towel him gently. He stared up at her, all eyes. He had the family colouring, brown hair and brown eyes, but his features were, as yet, indeterminate, his nose small and stubby, his mouth small and pink.

She kissed him on the tip of his nose. 'There you are—want some help getting dressed?'

'I'm going in to dress,' he said, retreating hurriedly.

'Fanny will dress him,' Angela told her with complacency. 'She loves to have them here for a little while; too much of them and she'd be climbing the walls, but once every now and then and she can enjoy the change.'

Dudley, Angela's husband, joined them a few minutes later and stood, towelling himself, exchanging polite remarks with Judith about her work, asking her how she was settling down in Doulton-Klein and telling her that he was a stockbroker himself.

'I don't know how you can stand it,' Angela told him, and to Judith said: 'Or you! It's such a dull life; some of Dudley's friends drive me scatty, I get toothache from trying not to yawn.'

Dudley was quite tall and very thin, Judith could see his ribs beneath his brown skin. He had fine dark hair and brown eyes and an angular, long-boned face. He seemed to find his wife enjoyable, he smiled at her teasingly. 'What Angela means is that she has a habit of going off to sleep halfway through an evening—she claims it's because my friends are so boring, but the truth is she's just a dormouse, she sleeps nine hours every night and still has to take a nap every afternoon.'

'Only when I'm pregnant,' Angela disputed.

Dudley looked at his watch. 'I'm going to get changed, coming up to the house, poppet?' This was to his daughter, not his wife, and Stephanie reluctantly dragged herself away from the sparkling blue water and padded over to join them, leaving wet footprints on the white tiles. When she had dried herself she and her father vanished and Angela groaned, forcing herself up to her feet.

'I suppose we'd better go too, or Fanny will start sending search parties down for us. She has a mania for punctuality, she sulks for days if anybody's late for a meal.'

They walked slowly back to the house, the sunshine warm on Judith's cheek and bare arms. 'My mother tells me she hasn't seen Baba since the engagement party,' Angela said suddenly. 'You know her quite well, I gather.'

'Yes,' Judith admitted warily, picking up something in Angela's tone that worried her.

'Is she really serious about Luke?'

Judith looked at Angela sharply. 'As far as I know—yes. Why?'

'Luke brought her down here once, that's all, he doesn't seem to see much of her. When mother asked him he told her Baba was away a good deal.'

'She is—she models abroad all the time.'

'It just seems a bit odd,' Angela said vaguely, frowning. 'I wondered if she was unsure about him. People who've just got engaged usually see a lot of each other.'

'I expect they will when Baba's not so busy,' Judith said defensively, although why she should feel compelled to rush to Baba's defence she did not know.

'It was all so sudden, he rushed into it; Mother says they've only known each other for a couple of months. She's worried about the whole thing.'

'Baba should be back any day, then she'll come down and see your mother, I'm sure.'

They went into the house a moment later and Angela vanished upstairs to get dressed. Judith heard some music in one of the rooms and walked towards it, expecting to find Dudley. She pushed the door wider and then stood frozen with shock on the threshold as Luke turned to look at her.

'You're not seeing things,' he assured her, laughing at her stunned surprise.

'When did you get back? I thought you were still in Sydney . . .'

'I flew back overnight.' He grinned. 'Can't you see that my eyes are propped open with matchsticks? I'm suffering from jet-lag, that's why I drove down here rather than go home. I need some peace and quiet. It never occurred to me that Angela and her brats would be here or I'd have shoved off to my flat.'

Judith pulled herself together, walking into the room with an assumed calm. 'Did everything go okay?' she asked.

'I think so.' He started to tell her about the meetings he had had in Sydney and while she listened she struggled to slow her heartbeat, quieten her pulse, get her high colour back under control. He was looking tired, there was no doubt about that; he was pale and there were shadows under his grey eyes. He was wearing a lightweight pale grey suit and a white silk shirt which was open at the throat and with which he wore no tie. She could see that he had recently shaved and his dark brown hair had a slight dampness at the temples, as though he had also just had a shower.

'I was tempted to come down for a swim when Fanny told me that was where you all were, but I needed a shave and a drink. I'll maybe have a swim later,' he said as Angela and Dudley arrived, turning towards them. 'Can I get you a drink, you two?'

'Pineapple juice for me, I'm not drinking because of the baby,' said Angela, lowering herself with care into a chair.

'I'll have a dry sherry,' Dudley decided.

Luke glanced at Judith, his brows lifting. 'Sorry—I forgot to ask you, what will you have?'

'The same, a dry sherry, thanks.'

They had just finished their drinks when Fanny came in with the children and said: 'Lunch is ready. Now!' she added as Luke moved towards the decanters arranged on a charming Georgian cabinet against the wall.

'I'm just putting my glass down,' Luke protested. He switched off the stereo which had been playing softly as they all talked and they filed out of the room, the two children attaching themselves to their father and chattering to him while their mother listened, smiling.

Lunch was a leisurely meal, and after it the adults went back into the pleasantly furnished sitting-room to drink coffee while the children vanished to talk to Fanny. Luke and his sister teased each other while Dudley smoked a cigar and sleepily watched them and Judith looked at the polished, antique furniture, the bowls of wallflowers and the pot of pink-petalled azaleas, the comfortable deep-upholstered brocade-covered chairs and sofas. It was a room to relax in, reassuringly traditional and filled with sunlight from the wide windows.

'We must be on our way soon,' said Dudley, looking at the gold-cased clock on the mantelpiece. It chimed three and they all turned to stare. 'It takes us an hour to get home from here,' he told Judith. 'When we've had tea and the kids have had their bath it's time to put them to bed. Sunday seems a much shorter day than any other—funny that, isn't it?'

A few minutes later he and Angela drove off with the children and Judith said reluctantly: 'I'd better go too.'

'Why?' Luke challenged. 'I was hoping you'd come for a swim—I'm going to have one now.'

Acutely aware of him, Judith shook her head quickly. 'I can't, I'm afraid, I didn't bring a costume with me.'

'So my mother told me. That's no problem. I've already seen to that—Angela keeps a few swimsuits here, I got Fanny to lay them out on her bed, you can take your pick. When she isn't pregnant, Angela is more or less your size, one of them is bound to fit you.'

Her face flushed with apprehension, Judith shook her head again. 'It's very kind of you to take the trouble, but I think I really ought to get back, I've got some work to finish before tomorrow.' She thought that that would let her off the hook, Luke would approve of her going back to work, but she was quite wrong, for he frowned at her.

'My mother has been scolding me for making you work so hard. She's right, too. I should have realised you were cramming yourself with all those folders, it's time you slowed down and took things more easily. We all need a little relaxation. Off you go; get changed and be down at the pool in ten minutes. You look as tired as I feel, some fresh air and exercise will be good for both of us.' He took her arm and pushed her towards the stairs, and Judith gave up trying to argue. She wanted to swim with him, why pretend she didn't? It was dangerous to her to be alone with him, especially in such intimacy, but she couldn't resist the chance and Luke had no idea how she felt, anyway; nothing would happen except that she would steal an hour or so of happiness. That wouldn't hurt Baba, the only one who might get hurt was herself.

She was taken aback when she looked at the swimsuits on the bed to find that they were all bikinis. That made her hesitate for a minute or so, but in the end she stripped off and put on a black bikini, then stood in front of the bedroom mirror staring at herself with nervous uneasiness.

The tiny cups left far too much of her pale breasts visible and the bikini briefs were tied at the hip with minute bows between which the dark material stretched tautly. It hardly seemed to her that she was wearing anything at all, she simply could not walk down through the garden to join Luke wearing something like this!

He tapped on the door before that thought had done more than flash through her head. 'Come on, I'll race you down there!'

Judith heard him running and opened her door to call: 'I've changed my mind . . .' but he was already out of earshot. She hesitated, then followed. She would dive into the pool as soon as she arrived, that way she wouldn't have to stand there while Luke looked at her.

When she emerged on the paved surround of the pool she saw his dark head in the water, his hair slickly plastered to his skull. He had his back to her as he swam, so she took advantage of that to run forward and dive off the side of the pool. Just as she leapt forward Luke turned to face in her direction. Judith was already hitting the blue water, she surfaced a second later and began to swim. She saw Luke's head a few feet away, rising and falling, sunlight glinting on the tanned stretch of his arms as he struck out.

The sun was now quite hot, it turned the pool to a dazzling sheet of light and Judith felt her shoulders absorbing the sun's rays as she stopped swimming and floated on her back, her eyes closed. Her wet hair drifted out from her head like sea weed, the buoyancy of the water made her body rise and fall without effort.

'Lazy,' scolded Luke, appearing beside her. 'Is that all you're going to do all afternoon?'

'Probably,' she said without opening her eyes.

She felt him floating beside her, his bare arm brushed hers and a fierce awareness shot through her, her eyes flew open and their gaze met. Luke's hard face was sombre, his mouth level. After a few seconds he looked from her eyes to her mouth and Judith felt the crash of her heartbeat shaking her whole body. They seemed to be locked in a strange silence, the rest of the world a million miles away. Luke's head moved closer, she watched his face, hypnotised, his mouth was coming down towards her own with such infinite slowness that it was like being in a slow motion film. She stopped thinking, she was shuddering with a need that hurt. Then Luke's lips touched her mouth and she jack-knifed abruptly, thrusting him away and at the same second turning on to her front to swim for the side.

She pulled herself out of the water and began to run. Luke caught her before she had got three paces. His hands fastened on to her bare, wet shoulders and whirled her round to face him.

'No, Luke . . .' she began before his mouth closed over her own again, opening her lips with a compelling heat before which she felt herself surrendering helplessly. She felt his fingers slide along her bare midriff, his hands moved on her wet back, one palm flattening against her waist to push her towards him while the other began to stroke along the smooth indentation of her spine, causing jagged splinters of mingled pleasure and pain to ache under her skin. She was trembling, shivering, conscious of his bare calves touching her legs, the roughness of the hair of his thighs pressed against her smoother skin. She tried to push him away, her hands on the broad, wet shoulders, but he was immovable. His fingers had reached the nape of her neck, he wound them into her tangled wet hair and pulled her head back, bent her slightly, her body shaped to fit beneath his, almost unbalancing her so that she could only cling to his shoulders to stay upright.

Luke lifted his mouth at last; with her eyes still shut she heard him say huskily: 'I've been wanting to do that for days.'

Her lashes were wet with tears, she opened her eyes and pushed him away angrily. 'You really are a bastard, aren't you? Baba's a friend of mine—I won't cheat on her, even if you're ready to!'

'I didn't intend that to happen, I wasn't planning to kiss you, but when you looked at me I . . .' he broke off, his mouth crooked. 'I'm so bloody jet-lagged I couldn't help it.'

'Do you have to try it on with every woman you meet? My God, if I looked like Baba I might understand you making a pass, but don't try to kid me you find me irresistible! I'm not that dumb.' Her face was stinging with angry colour. 'I don't like having routine passes made at me!'

'You're not dumb, you're plain crazy,' Luke said wearily. 'Don't tell me you don't know how I feel, because I've seen you look at me—I know you've noticed, you're too clever not to have realised.'

Judith didn't feel clever; she felt bewildered. She stared at him, her dark eyes wide, searching his face for clues. What was he talking about?

'I'm not going to apologise for falling in love with you.' He was looking at her in a way that made her heart flop over in sickening happiness. 'I'm a realist. It's happened and there's nothing I can do about it, nothing I want to do about it.'

'You can't,' she protested. 'I'm not beautiful, like Baba, I'm . . .'

'Even if you were so ugly you had to go around with a bag over your head, I'd still want to be with you all the time,' Luke interrupted with a sudden smile. 'Beautiful? No, my love, you're not beautiful—but then that isn't what I love about you, how you look. It's how you think. I love your sharpness and quickness, your sense of humour, your cool way of looking at things. I proposed to Baba on a crazy impulse. I wanted a wife. She was everything I'd thought I was looking for—she was beautiful and kind and sweet-tempered, she didn't seem to have any flaws at all. So I rushed into a proposal and everyone seemed pleased; my mother was delighted, Angela liked her, it was all perfect.' He turned his head, brushing back a wet strand of hair from his face, his eyes miserable. 'Until I met you, and fell in love and realised that I'd made a hellish mistake.'

CHAPTER EIGHT

JUDITH was stiff with shock, her skin icy, she had to sit
down before her legs gave way beneath her. She
stumbled to a lounger and practically fell on to it. Luke
sat on the lounger next to her.

'How was I to know I was going to walk into you
five minutes after getting engaged to her?' he said, more
to himself than her. 'If I'd never asked her to marry me,
I'd never have met you anyway—that's the ironic part.
Whoever arranges these things has a perverted sense of
humour. One minute I was feeling quite pleased with
life because Baba seemed to be exactly what I'd been
looking for—the next I was in the middle of that fight
with you at the nightclub, and that was when you
started getting under my skin. I was ready to break
things when you looked at me as if you thought I was a
rat. I told myself it didn't matter a damn what you
thought, but I knew it did. I should have been warned,
then, but it still didn't dawn on me . . .'

Judith had stopped trembling now, she sat up,
swallowing to clear her throat. 'I think we'd better go
back to the house and get dressed now and I'd better
leave. We'll pretend this discussion never happened,
and as soon as I can, I'll find another job.' She had
thought out what she was going to say before she said
it; her voice sounded calm and level and her face, she
hoped, gave the same impression, although she was not
so sure of that. She did know, however, that facts were
facts—she had been drumming that into herself since
she was very small and they told her that her father was
dead. From that moment she had been on her own,

although at the time she hadn't understood that. It was only gradually that she had realised that her father's death had shattered her family life. After that, her mother was never there and her grandparents were so old. The symmetry of the family had been destroyed overnight. Family life protects children from the cold winds of reality, she thought; most people don't realise until long after they have become adults that everyone is essentially alone in life. Judith had never that sort of shelter after her father died; she had envied other children their normal family backgrounds. She remembered vividly hearing her mother say: 'I must go out to work now, of course. Facts are facts, you can't change them by wishing.' It must have been embedded in her consciousness by the pain of the moment; from then on she had made herself face facts. She had to face them now.

'You can't back out of your marriage now; you'd hurt Baba too much,' she said.

'It would hurt her a damn sight more to be married to me when I love you.'

'She mustn't know.'

'You can't be serious,' he said, sitting up in a violent movement, his body stiff with denial.

'Love doesn't last for ever, you could fall out of love with me one day.' Each word hurt, but she made herself say them.

'I think I fell in love with you the minute I saw you . . .'

'The first time you saw me you didn't even notice what I looked like,' she said, and he stared at her angrily. 'We met in New York last autumn and you haven't even remembered . . .'

Luke looked confused. 'Last autumn? Did we? When?'

'We weren't introduced,' she told him. 'I noticed you—but you certainly didn't even look twice at me.'

'That doesn't alter anything,' he said. 'Judith, I love you now.'

Judith was making herself think about Baba when she really wanted to hear Luke say again that he loved her; the words still beat in her ears, in her bloodstream, she had never thought she would ever hear him say that to her. She still couldn't quite believe he meant it, it was so hard to believe, but she couldn't refuse to believe in the tension she saw in his face, the piercing angularity of his facial bones beneath the damp brown skin. Luke was serious, he hadn't just been flirting with her when he kissed her just now; if he had smiled or tried to go on making love to her she might have doubted him, but his voice was so harsh and strained, he was so angry and miserable. That look on his face was the truth; there was no mistaking it.

'I don't know whether love lasts for ever or not,' Luke said fiercely, 'I only know it isn't possible for me to marry Baba now. She's too nice for me to do that to her—I'd really be cheating her if I went through with marrying her. It's my fault; I went into our engagement without meaning a damn thing I said to her. I thought it was enough to enjoy being with her, I didn't expect there were ever be anything else. I was ready to settle for second best, I thought I'd make her happy and that that was all that mattered. If I'd known . . . but I didn't, how could I have guessed that you were just around the next corner?'

'Don't!' Judith said sharply, getting up abruptly. She wanted to hear what he was saying, but she wanted it too much, her own intensity frightened her.

Luke leapt up too and caught her before she could move; his arms round her. She felt the heavy beating of his heart against her breasts; her body shuddered in his nearness.

'I'm a different person now,' he told her. 'Before I

met you my whole life was like a millpond, nothing much bothered me, it was so peaceful and ordinary. I had it all neatly arranged; I went to the office in my car every morning and had meetings with people or went through business with my secretary. I read my paper and over lunch I talked to whoever I was with, then I went back to the office and got on with more work, and I went home and showered and changed and had dinner, in or out. Theatres, board-rooms, planes to the States or Switzerland or Tokyo. Every day I was busy and every day it was the same; nothing stirred on the surface of my millpond. I was perfectly contented. The only flaw in my life was that I'd never got around to getting married, so I decided to do something about that. I wanted children, I promised my mother I'd give her some grandchildren. It seemed simple enough. Find a nice girl, marry her and get on with living the way I always had. As soon as I started looking around I saw Baba and thought: she'll do.' He moved his cheek slowly against Judith's wet hair. 'It serves me right for being such an arrogant, stupid fool. I wasn't really bothered whether Baba loved me or not; she was suitable, she'd do. I'm rich, I can buy whatever I want. That's how I thought, and I deserve the trouble I've bought myself.'

'I won't argue with that,' Judith said huskily. She was aching to put her arms round his neck, she didn't want him to talk, she wanted him to touch her and she was longing to touch him, her hands were trembling with a desire to stroke his strong face, move over the muscular tanned chest which was touching her.

'You hit my millpond like a tidal wave—I'm still crashing about,' Luke told her, his arms tightening. 'I guess I knew I loved you when we were playing croquet here that day; when you laugh it makes me feel so crazily happy. I didn't want that day to end. I didn't want you to go. While I've been away I've counted the hours until I could ring you again; hearing your voice was the only thing that kept me from flying back here and abandoning the negotiations. I'd have offended those guys over there and blown a hole right in the middle of my current plans, but if I hadn't been able to talk to you every day I'd have risked all that and come back to you.'

'Luke, don't,' she whispered. 'This isn't doing any good; the fact is you're engaged to Baba, she has no idea you aren't in love with her, and even if you did break off your engagement, I couldn't possibly marry you—Baba would never forgive me, I'd never forgive myself for having stolen you from her.'

He put a hand under her chin, forcing her head up so that he could see her face. 'You can't steal what never belonged to her in the first place. I didn't love her.'

'She doesn't know that. She thinks you do—and she loves you; she told me she was crazy about you.'

Luke's face paled and stiffened.

'Baba would be so hurt,' Judith said unhappily. 'I couldn't do that to her, Luke. I'd never be able to live with it. I'm just not that sort of person. My conscience would give me no peace, we wouldn't be happy.'

'Darling,' he muttered, the word pleading, forced out of him and so deep that his voice sounded agonised.

'Let me go, Luke,' she asked as levelly as she could. The physical contact was torture, she couldn't take any more of it.

He looked at her in silence for a moment, his fingers biting into the soft skin under her chin.

'I must go,' she whispered. 'I must.'

'Not yet,' Luke said thickly. His head lowered, his mouth met hers with a demand she couldn't fight off and, in spite of her attempt to remain passive under that angry kiss, she felt her lips parting, quivering in response. The next second her eyes were closing, her body melting in a pleasure whose intensity defeated all her reasoned defences against him.

This will be the last time, she told herself; never again. Giving herself that promise made it disastrously easy for her to give in to her own feelings; she touched Luke at last, openly caressing the strong shoulders and powerful chest. An arm slid round his neck, she curved closer, stroking the ends of his thick hair where they lay damply against the nape of his neck. Luke slid her strap down and she felt his hand take possession of her naked breast; her skin burned as he touched it, the warm flesh filling with excited blood, and an intense sexual hunger ran through her entire body. Trembling, she pulled her head back, almost too breathless to speak, shaking her head as she pulled up her bikini strap again.

'No; Luke, no!'

His hands dropped away, she heard him breathing audibly, sharply. Judith walked away unsteadily. It seemed to take her years to get back to the house; Luke didn't follow her. She went upstairs and got changed, brushed her hair slowly with a shaking hand and put on some new make-up. Before she drove back to London she would have to say goodbye to Mrs Doulton and she didn't know how she was going to face her; she was terrified that Luke's mother might be able to read what had just happened in her face. It was a terrible relief to find Fanny lurking about outside Mrs Doulton's room and be told in a sulky voice that Mrs Doulton was asleep.

'Will you give her my love and say I had to get back?' Judith asked with a pretence of calm.

Fanny grudgingly agreed. Judith turned away from the other woman's sharp eyes. Fanny had stared at her; she couldn't guess, of course, how should she? But Judith felt uneasy under that penetrating stare.

She drove back to London much faster than she normally drove; she wanted to be sure of getting back before Luke could catch up with her. She didn't think he would follow, but she wasn't a hundred per cent sure about it and she was in no fit state to face any more confrontation. Next time she might not have the courage to walk away.

Her flat seemed small and very quiet. She sat curled up on her bed for a few moments, thinking about Luke; it was still too new, too unbelievable, to be thought about without numb incredulity. Everything he had said, every look in his face, had been burned into her memory, it might be all she had to carry with her into a blank future. She put her hands over her face. He loves me, she thought. It can't be true, I want it to be true so much—her heart turned over and over, she was one minute icy cold, the next feverishly hot. Judith had spent her whole life forcing herself to accept reality, she wasn't ready, now, to believe that dreams could become reality. In her mind there was a sharp division between the two of them—dreams were moonlit passages between day and day, they were the secret crevices of the mind where she hid what she would not think about in her waking hours. For weeks now she had met Luke in her stupid dreams and woken up to know just what a fool she was, how could she allow herself to accept that he was, after all, within her reach? She could be happy—if she chose, but only by taking happiness from someone else. The price was too high.

It was dusk, almost night, and the moths began to tap at the windows as she switched on the light and forgot to draw the curtains. Her thoughts fluttered helplessly, like that, trying to force their way through the implacable glass between pain and joy.

To make herself feel normal, she rang her grandmother. 'Did you have a good day in Kent?' Mrs Murry asked, completely unaware of the turmoil inside Judith.

'It was quite hot,' Judith told her. 'They have a swimming pool—we all swam.'

'We? I thought you said Mrs Doulton was bedridden.'

'Her daughter Angela was there, with her husband and their children. She's expecting a third baby.' Judith talked about Angela for a while, her voice was still breathless and shaky, but she hoped her grandmother might not pick that up.

'What exactly is wrong with Mrs Doulton?' Mrs Murry asked.

'I'm not sure—she has a very weak heart, she told me, but she also has some sort of hip trouble, I think she had an operation on her hip a few months ago and it went wrong. She doesn't talk about her illness much and I don't like to ask too many questions. She's always so cheerful and lively, it's hard to believe she's seriously ill, but Luke . . .' She stopped because even saying his name had dangers, she was afraid of what she might betray to her grandmother.

'When does he get back from Australia?' asked Mrs Murry, and Judith moistened her dry lips before she replied.

'He's back.' She tried to sound casual. 'Got back today.'

'Oh, he was down there, was he?' her grandmother asked in a quick, sharp voice.

'Yes.'

'How much longer is Baba going to be away?' Mrs Murry asked. What was she thinking? Judith hated to imagine.

'No idea. Ruth hasn't heard from her.'

'I don't understand young people today; they seem to behave in a very offhand way. Those two hardly seem to have seen each other since they got engaged; Baba shot off almost at once. It looks to me as though this is going to be a very long-distance marriage.'

Judith murmured something vague and a moment later rang off. She wasn't hungry, she couldn't concentrate on her work, she made herself watch television for an hour, but once she was in bed couldn't remember anything she had seen. It had been so much moving wallpaper for her to stare at blankly while her mind relived those moments down by the swimming pool. Catching herself at it, she grew angry. She must not let herself think about it, about Luke; she must put all such thoughts out of her head. If she gave in to her own craving to remember his mouth, his hands, the way he had looked at her, she would only be storing up trouble for herself later. Love was like an insidious disease, you didn't fight it by giving in to it; you drove it out using every weapon you had; however unpleasant the cure, the disease was far worse.

When she went in to work next day she was coldly tired; she hadn't slept and she knew it showed. Her dark eyes had shadows under them, her mouth lay in a weary curve. She was dreading seeing Luke, she trembled as she got up to their floor in the building, expecting him to emerge from his office or walk into her own at any moment.

Her secretary, Janice, came in with a pile of post and put it in Judith's in-tray with a smile. 'Good morning, Miss Murry. Did you know that Mr Doulton's back? He left a message to say he was taking the Christopher meeting himself and you needn't show up. He should be back around three, he said. He has a lunch appointment with Sir Henry Morton and he'll raise that matter of the platinum shares then.' Janice looked up from her notebook, having read that from her shorthand. 'So you've got the morning free.'

'Is this what you call freedom?' Judith asked drily,

lifting the dozens of letters from her in-tray. 'We might as well go through these now—sit down, Janice.'

Janice pulled a chair forward and sat down. She was a slim, attractive girl of twenty-two with smooth brown hair and blue eyes; not particularly pretty but with a lively smile which could make her seem pretty at times. She was always calm and cheerful, her job wasn't very important to her, Judith had gathered, she planned to get married in a year or so to a trainee architect with whom she had been going out for years. They had been at school together. Judith didn't get the impression that Janice was madly in love, but she was quietly happy with her young man.

They worked for an hour on the letters, then the phone rang and Janice answered it. Looking up, she said softly: 'It's Mr Howell from Span Plastics, he's been trying to talk to Mr Doulton for days, he says. Will you talk to him?'

Judith considered her thoughtfully. 'No, tell him I'm in a meeting.' Span was one of the companies Luke was currently buying into and she knew that his appearance on their horizon had put the fear of God into the board; she did not want to discuss Luke's plans with one of the directors.

Luke's chief accountant came in to see her just before lunch, a box folder in his arms. 'Time to go through these with me?' he enquired hopefully, and she made a wry face.

'What is it?' Ralph Golding was a persistent man obsessed with figures and graphs; he had been working with Luke for years and had spent five years over in the States familiarising himself with that side of Doulton-Klein. He was very definitely a power in the organisation and he knew it; Judith had rapidly realised that she had to get Ralph on her side if she wasn't to have trouble. Like any large organisation, Doulton-

Klein was split into various lobbies who each had particular axes to grind and who pursued petty vendettas with each other in subtle ways which made them hard to pin down and defeat. Judith had met that sort of thing before at the bank she had worked at until she joined Luke; she knew the wisdom of staying neutral if you could.

'I'm just taking soundings,' Ralph said smoothly, sitting down and opening his box folder. 'Trying this out on people before I take it to Luke—best to iron out all the problems first and it helps to get a new eye on the subject.'

Judith looked grimly at her own work, then pushed it aside. 'Go ahead,' she said with as much calm as she could muster. She couldn't afford to offend Ralph.

By the time he left she only had half an hour for lunch, she sent Janice out for some sandwiches and fruit and ate at her desk. Janice was gone over an hour, she was meeting her fiancé.

Judith had a meeting that afternoon. Luke wasn't involved and it was nearly six before she went back to her office. Janice was just covering her typewriter. She gave Judith a sympathetic smile.

'You look worn out.'

'I am—any messages?'

'Mr Doulton dropped by, I told him where you were and he said it wasn't important, he'd catch you tomorrow. Span Plastics rang again, so did Mr Wilkins . . .' Janice ran through a long list of telephone calls and Judith nodded, making an occasional note on her pad when a call had to be returned quickly.

When Janice finished Judith asked: 'Letters go off okay?'

'Yes—was there anything you wanted before I left?'

Judith shook her head. 'I'm going home myself shortly. See you tomorrow, Janice.'

'If I were you I'd have a long bath and go to bed,' Janice told her. 'You're tired, anyone can see that, you need a good night's sleep.'

'I'll make sure I get one,' Judith said drily. Janice smiled at her and went, and Judith sat down behind her desk, contemplating the mass of folders she should take home and study. She had never felt less like work in her life. She had kept thoughts of Luke at bay by working herself into the ground; now she felt dead.

She debated whether to take the paperwork home or leave it, then with a sigh knew she had to take it—she still hadn't caught up with all the ramifications of her job and if she left the outer limits of it untouched she probably wouldn't ever quite understand what was going on in the organisation.

That night she drugged herself to sleep with massive doses of work. When she put the light out at eleven she felt like a zombie and fell asleep almost at once, slept heavily all night and woke up when her alarm went off with a shriek that sent her leaping out of bed before she even knew she was awake. Dazedly she stumbled into the kitchen, put on the kettle, trudged into the bathroom and showered in half-cold water that at least opened her eyes fully, towelled herself vigorously and went to get dressed, after she had rushed to the kitchen to make some tea. When she sat down to eat a slice of toast and a boiled egg she felt more human. Her copy of the *Financial Times* arrived as she was eating her egg; she was able to read its pink pages while she was drinking her tea and nibbling some toast and marmalade. She hadn't eaten last night and her lunch had been tiny; she was hungry.

There was a large policy meeting that morning; Luke was already there when Judith arrived. She was nervous, it would be the first time she had seen him since she walked away from him in his mother's garden.

He was listening to one of the other executives with a frown, but as Judith walked through the door Luke turned his head, his gaze shooting across the room, and she knew he had sensed her arrival. It made her so tense to know that he was as aware of her presence as she was aware of his that she could hardly manage a polite smile when someone else said: 'Hallo, Judith, you look very elegant.'

'Thanks,' she said, feeling Luke listening. She was wearing a lemon silk shirt and a pale grey skirt with a broad leather belt. She looked cool and immaculate; it was an image she had decided to project this morning. It wouldn't give away too much of the turmoil inside her.

During the long meeting Luke at one time passed a letter to her. 'Have you seen this?' he said levelly, but Judith felt his fingertips brush her hand and she couldn't meet his eyes.

'No,' she said. It was the first time she had spoken directly to him. It amazed her that all the others were so blind to what was going on; they hadn't picked up anything odd between Luke and herself, obviously nothing showed, yet she felt so screwed up that her facial bones ached.

She left the meeting just before twelve. She felt Luke walking behind her; his stare seemed to be fixed somewhere between her shoulder blades, but someone was with him, talking rapidly, he had to let her walk away.

She went through some letters with Janice until lunch time, then shot out of her office to drive across London to a lunch with someone with one of the major banks. It was four o'clock when she got back, and as she parked her car in the underground car park she saw Robert getting out of his own car.

'What are *you* doing here?' she asked, smiling, as he

walked over to join her by the lift. His footsteps rang in the high-ceilinged concrete vault; if he hadn't been smiling it would have given him an air of menace.

'I'm here for a meeting with your Mr Aldridge.'

'Aldridge,' she thought aloud. She hadn't yet familiarised herself with the names of all the executive staff. Hundreds of people worked in the Doulton-Klein building; probably she never would know all of them even by name.

'Overseas Development,' he prompted, and then the name rang a faint bell. Judith nodded, smiling. 'I'm early,' Robert admitted. 'I'm on my way back from another appointment and there seemed no point in wasting time going to the office first. I thought I might get a cup of coffee from Aldridge's secretary if I had to wait.'

'Come to my office, we'll find you some coffee,' she promised.

'How hospitable!' Robert mocked, laughing.

'We try to make our friends happy.' They stepped out of the lift and she stopped off at Janice's little office to say: 'Make some coffee for two, would you, Janice?' Then she and Robert went into her own office and she sat down behind the desk and waved a hand at the chair in front of it. 'Sit down, Robert.'

He was looking around, his face wry. 'Very impressive. You're obviously highly thought of to get an office this big—you were very wise to come here instead of coming to us. I doubt if we could have given you anything bigger than a cardboard box.'

It was a very large, elegantly furnished office, far bigger than she had ever expected to be given; the carpet was a soothing creamy beige and the windows were masked by slatted blinds which she could use to keep out the sunlight on a very hot day, the furniture was modern and expensive and on the matt blue walls hung a few beautifully reproduced prints of modern paintings. It had the air of being more of a sitting-room than an office, it was a place in which you could relax— if you ever had the time and no mound of work to get through.

Robert perched on the edge of her desk and scanned the paperwork on her desk briefly. 'Do you get much aggro from the men? Much backbiting because you got the job and they didn't?'

'If they have dark thoughts they keep them to themselves. I'm not the only female assistant Luke has—he has several in the States, too.' Judith had talked to them on the phone now; they seemed to be older than herself and they had been with Luke for some time, she had picked up a certain amount of possessive self-interest in the way they talked about him.

'We all know he likes women,' Robert said drily. He sauntered around the desk to look out of the window. 'Not much of a view.'

'I wouldn't have time to look at it anyway.'

'You work too hard,' said Robert, bending over her chair to kiss her, so suddenly that she only just had time to move away before he did. He froze, staring at her, flushing, and she regretted her hurried duck away.

'I'm sorry, Robert,' she stammered while he looked at her in that hurt surprise, and at that moment the door opened and they both looked, guiltily, towards the door, expecting to see Janice with the coffee. Instead they saw Luke.

He stood on the threshold, looking at them, his lean face harsh. Judith went scarlet, then white, she saw his lips fasten into a tight line and his nostrils flare angrily. She knew he had caught something in the atmosphere between herself and Robert.

'Hallo, Luke,' Robert said uneasily, dragging a smile into his face.

Luke gave him a curt nod. He kept his eyes on Judith as he did so, only flicking a brief glance Robert's way. 'I want to talk to you, Miss Murry. My office in five minutes.'

He went out, closing the door very quietly.

'Aren't you allowed to have callers?' Robert asked jokily, but he gave her a curious, puzzled look.

'I'm here to work, remember,' Judith said as lightly as she could. Janice came in with the coffee and a worried, uncertain smile.

'Mr Doulton asked me to let him know when you got back, I didn't expect him to come himself, I just phoned his secretary and told her you'd arrived and the next minute he . . .'

'That's okay, Janice,' Judith said reassuringly.

'He seemed to be angry about something,' Janice added, lingering.

'Obviously something has gone wrong,' said Judith, getting up. 'I'd better go and find out. Stay and drink your coffee, Robert. I'll get Janice to ring Aldridge and tell him you're in the building and will be up soon.'

'Free for dinner tonight?' Robert asked as she walked to the door, and she turned with a polite smile, shaking her head.

'Sorry, I'm so busy . . .'

'Another time, then,' said Robert, and she nodded. She was shaking as she walked along the corridor to Luke's office; she paused outside, breathing deeply to calm herself, then tapped and at his brusque: 'Come in,' opened the door.

He was standing by the window with his back to her. 'Close the door,' he said without turning, and she knew he was perfectly well aware that it was her. 'What was Gordon doing in your office? What was going on?' Luke demanded, and as she hesitated for an answer turned to face her, his grey eyes filled with icy hostility.

'I know you've been dating him, but I don't like the idea of having him snooping around your office and taking a look at all the private documents lying around on your desk. You're not to have the man there again, is that understood? You have a very confidential job, I would have thought it was obvious that someone like Gordon shouldn't be running loose around the office.'

'He only came in for a cup of coffee; he didn't look at any of the papers.'

'What was he doing when I came in? You both jumped about six feet in the air—I've never seen such guilty expressions!' He was biting out the words between his teeth, a dark red colour in his face. Judith shrank from the anger in those grey eyes; there was violence in the air, distaste in the way he spoke.

'We were startled, that's all.'

'Startled? It looked to me as if you were in his arms until I opened the door.'

Her own temper flared. 'If I had been that wouldn't be any of your business! My private life is my own affair. I'll make sure Robert never sees any confidential papers, but . . .'

Luke moved abruptly and she shrank, fumbling with the door handle. He stood right in front of her, looking down at her. 'For God's sake, Judith . . .'

'Don't!' she broke out as he caught her shoulders.

'I was jealous,' he said huskily, his fingers tightening on the slender bones he held.

'You had no right . . .'

'That makes it worse—I couldn't even punch his face for him, I had to pretend to be polite.'

'*That* I didn't notice!' said Judith with a spurt of angry laughter. Was that what he called pretending to be polite? Looking at poor, bewildered Robert as though he was a slug he had just discovered in his lettuce?

'I suddenly realised you could see him, let him kiss you, and there as nothing I could do about it,' Luke said in a thick, harsh voice. 'I want to tell the world you're mine, I don't want to have to stand back and watch you with other men, that would drive me slowly round the bend . . .'

'I'd better leave then,' said Judith through what seemed to be a mouthful of broken glass. Every syllable hurt, but she said them, feeling Luke's fingers bite into her as he heard the words. He was white now, she saw lines around his eyes and mouth as he struggled for control.

'You can't,' he said. 'I couldn't bear it, I'd miss you so much I wouldn't want to live.' He bent his head and she felt his lips against her throat. His voice whispered beneath her ear. 'I want to be with you all day; you aren't smiling at me, any more; I thought when I got back to London it would be enough just to talk to you, work with you, watch that smile in your eyes—but everything is going wrong; you're not with me, you're so distant. I tried to see you all day yesterday and you were never here and today you've been avoiding me— tell me the truth, darling. Is it all on my side? Don't you care, after all? I thought you did, I thought it was the same for you as me; was I fooling myself?'

She closed her eyes and ached with a pain deeper than she had ever known. 'I can't, Luke.' Why had he met Baba first. Why had he asked her to marry him when he didn't love her?

He was rigid, she couldn't see his face, it was buried against her neck, but his lips were icy and his breathing now was shallow and jerky.

'You don't love me?' he asked, and she tried to lie to him, to tell him she didn't, but she could not force the words between her lips. Her heart would not let her lie to him.

Luke lifted his head after a long moment and looked into her eyes. Judith tore herself away, walked into the centre of the room with her back to him. 'It won't work if you don't stay away from me,' she said. 'I'll have to leave if this sort of thing happens again.'

Luke walked round his desk and sat down. He put his dark head between his hands and sat in silence and after a moment Judith left. There was nothing they could say to each other.

The incident didn't make it any easier to work with him. Luke kept his distance now, he stayed strictly on the business level, but it was torture for Judith to be in the same room day after day and to feel Luke's awareness of her at every minute. Even though he didn't try to touch her again, or mention anything but work, there were unavoidable moments when their hands brushed or they stood next to each other in a lift or were alone in an office for an hour. Judith felt each second of those moments; she was conscious of her own hidden emotions and could guess at his, she watched the deft movement of his long-fingered hands as he flicked over a page, observed the tension of his cheekbones when he looked down, the unsteadiness of his mouth as he looked up again and caught her watching him, heard the husky note in his voice with a constricted heart. Once his knee touched her own and she took a quick breath. Luke looked at her sideways, a fever in his eyes. Dry-mouthed, she bent her head and pretended to read the paper in front of her. She had often pushed herself to the limit as far as work was concerned, that was nothing new to her—but now she was pushing both of them beyond the limits of human endurance and each day the sensual torture seemed to intensify. It almost seemed to have become an exquisite pleasure; the higher the barriers between them the more achingly she longed to cross them, and the more she wanted to touch Luke, feel his mouth on hers, the higher the screw of pain was turned until it passed the level at which pain was pleasure. She only became aware of that when she realised how closely she was flirting with danger; she was now deliberately seeing him alone, watching him, letting their hands touch. The more it hurt the more she enjoyed it. Neither she nor Luke ever mentioned what was happening, but she strongly suspected Luke was going through the same process. She knew he watched her, she knew he stood behind her chair in the board room and bent over to look at one of the folders in front of her, his cheek an inch from hers, she was well aware that he went out of his way to put a hand on her shoulder or her arm, give her a cup of coffee, brush a buzzing wasp away from her neck. If any other man had done any of those things she would barely have noticed. They were both using intimate, familiar moments like weapons to hurt each other because they could not reach each other any other way.

During her fourth week with Doulton-Klein she rang Ruth to ask when Baba was coming back, and Ruth said in surprise: 'Didn't Luke tell you? She should be back on Saturday. She's had her tests and now she's waiting to hear for certain whether or not she's got the part. She rang me a few nights ago. She was terribly excited. Apparently she's staying with the director at his house—Baba says he has a fabulous swimming pool and there are fifteen rooms in the house and three of them are bathrooms. He has a jacuzzi and a solarium and an enormous barbecue patio. Baba says he has parties every single night.'

'Sounds like fun,' Judith said jerkily. 'She has told Luke she's coming back, has she?'

'Oh, yes, she said she's rung him lots of times. He keeps pressing her to come back, she said. Well, she can't be surprised about that—she's been away for ages and it isn't fair on Luke, but I think she's been having such a great time over there that she didn't want to come back. It's been like a simply fabulous holiday; all expenses paid. She said she had three different tests and . . .'

'Is this director married?' Judith interrupted, and Ruth giggled.

'Just between you and me, that's what I asked her—but he is, and his wife's a darling, Baba said, she gets on with her like a house on fire. It was his wife who asked Baba to stay with them, the hotel was so huge that Baba got lost when she tried to find her room.'

Judith sighed. 'That was nice of them. American hotels are much bigger than ours—some of them have a thousand rooms.'

'Help! No wonder Baba wanted to get out of it. She's keeping her fingers crossed about the part—as she's only done some amateur acting up to now the producer was dubious about giving it to her, but now that he's seen all her tests she thinks he may just change his mind.'

Why hadn't Luke told her that Baba was coming home soon? Judith wondered as she put the phone down later. She sat staring at nothing, her face pale. She had to get a new job, that was obvious. It was going to be a bit difficult to explain why she should suddenly leave such a highly paid, high status job after only a short while. She was never going to get anything as good, she had to face that. But she knew she would not be able to stand the torture of being with Luke all day after he had married Baba. That would just send her quietly out of her mind.

CHAPTER NINE

MRS DOULTON rang Judith next morning just as she was dashing out to a meeting. 'I wondered if you could come down this weekend, Judith—I haven't seen you for some time and I enjoy our little chats. Could you drive down on Sunday?'

Judith hesitated; she would have loved to go, but she was afraid of finding Luke there. 'Well, I . . .'

'Would it be too boring for you? I suppose it must be, it's been good of you to put up with all my anecdotes about people you've never met,' Mrs Doulton said, picking up her hesitation and mis-interpreting it.

'I love talking to you,' Judith denied quickly. 'It's just that I have to see my grandmother this weekend—I rarely get a chance to visit her during the week, I'm too busy. I thought I'd take her out on Sunday; now that I have a car, you see, I can drive her to the sea or into the country, it gives her a change of scenery.'

'Bring her here,' Mrs Doulton said at once as though under the impression that that was what Judith had been hinting at, and Judith stammered: 'Oh, I couldn't . . . I mean . . . it's kind of you, but you don't even know her . . .' She was horrified, caught between two fires, she did not want to hurt or offend Mrs Doulton, but she equally did not want to go down and visit her, running the risk of seeing Luke.

'I'd like to know her,' said Mrs Doulton, laughing. 'From what you've told me about her I think we'll take to each other. At least ask her if she'll come, will you, Judith?' and, of course Judith had to say she would.

Judith had a very shrewd idea of her grandmother's character and how she would react in any situation; Mrs Murry was obstinate and unsociable, she did not like strangers, she was bound to refuse to go down to Lambourne to visit Luke's mother. Judith didn't feel too worried about promising Mrs Doulton that she would pass on the invitation; she would be amazed if it was accepted.

'I'll let you know if we can come,' she said before she rang off. 'Will your daughter and her children be there?' She dared not ask if Luke was going to come; that would be too much of a giveaway.

'They may drop in—I'm never sure if they will or not, it depends what else is happening. Angela's husband often has visitors for lunch on a Sunday and then they don't drive over to see me.' Mrs Doulton paused, then said: 'And Luke can't get down, either. He's flying to Paris on Friday night, isn't he?'

'Is he? I've no idea,' said Judith with a sense of wild relief. Was Luke going to be away long? She didn't know whether to hope he was or to fear it; she would miss him, but at the same time she would be able to breathe more easily if he wasn't around for a while.

When she mentioned the invitation to her grandmother on the phone that night Mrs Murry unpredictably sounded quite excited. 'I'd love to go, I've been dying to see this lovely house for myself.'

'It's a long drive,' Judith warned, taken aback. Of course, Luke wouldn't be around, she wouldn't be running the risk of being alone with him again, but she still felt unwilling to go because the place would always remind her of those moments when Luke kissed her and told her that he loved her. She was trying very hard not to remember the piercing happiness she had felt then.

'I'm not senile, a long drive won't kill me,' Mrs Murry protested, very offended.

On the Friday evening Judith came out of her office to make her way to the lift and met Luke bound the same way. Some of the office staff were in the corridor; both Judith and Luke smiled politely at them and each other. It was such a farce—Judith was tempted to laugh at their pretences except that she didn't find it funny, either her sense of humour had gone on the blink or the nagging pain inside her made it quite impossible to laugh at anything.

Luke was carrying a tan leather suitcase. She looked at it, asking: 'Going away for the weekend?' as if she had no idea he was off to Paris, and Luke nodded.

'I'm combining business with pleasure and spending a couple of days over in Paris. I'm seeing René Larchain for lunch tomorrow.'

She nodded. 'Well, good luck with him—on the phone and in his letters he sounds very tricky.'

Luke's mouth was wry. 'He is,' he agreed, and his brief glance at her reminded her how well he knew the man. 'But I'll manage,' Luke added, and she was sure he would.

They went down in the lift together. It was so crowded that she was forced into the corner and felt Luke's hip touching hers all the way down, aware of his dark sleeve brushing her breast as he shifted to make more room. Most of the office staff got out on the ground floor, they would be taking trains or buses home, but Luke and Judith went down to the underground car park two floors below. They walked side by side towards the bay in which their cars were parked; each department had its own bay. The shadows and sudden crude pools of yellow light from the overhead strip lighting made the place ominous, Judith heard their footsteps echoing on the concrete walls. Luke paused beside his own car, looking at her.

'Have a good weekend. Try to relax, you're like a

piece of stretched elastic lately. Take the whole weekend off, don't do any work at all.' His voice was rough, his hand moved to touch her arm, then fell again.

'Have a good time in Paris,' said Judith, equally husky, and Luke got into his car. He was already driving away before she had switched on the ignition; she sat and watched the orange flare of his tail lights vanishing before following him up the steep ramp into the daylight.

Next day she did the weekend shopping and had coffee in the pedestrian precinct near her flat, went back to do her housework and then had lunch and spent the rest of the day with her grandmother. It was fine, a warm summer day; Judith sunbathed in a deckchair while Mrs Murry pottered about among the roses; cutting off withered heads and dropping them into a wicker trug, bending to sniff the scent of the opening white and crimson buds. Judith closed her eyes and let the tranquillity seep into her bones; she was so tired she found it hard to relax, to let go of the various pressures which had been driving her all week. She had had to screw herself up to face them and now it wasn't easy to slacken and unwind; she felt slightly dizzy. When Luke gave her that job she knew he had flung her a challenge which she hadn't wanted to refuse. The work was difficult, she hadn't had any real idea how testing it was—it had taken her almost a month to work herself into the job, but she knew she had done it. The hours and hours of relentless paperwork were paying off. She might have found it much easier if her life had not been complicated by having fallen in love with Luke; she felt as if she had been caught in a vice for weeks. Her jaws ached with weariness.

'I think I'll take some of these roses down to Mrs Doulton,' her grandmother murmured. 'I suppose she has masses of flowers in her garden.'

'Masses,' Judith agreed, then opened her eyes and smiled at Mrs Murry. 'But I've no doubt she'd love to get your roses, she has flowers everywhere in the house. It would be a nice gesture.'

Next morning they set off to drive to Kent. Mrs Murry carefully laid a huge bunch of roses on the back seat; she had cut them earlier and Judith saw among the dark red petals the odd glassy drop of dew. The fragrance of the flowers soon filled the car as the day grew warmer, she opened the windows wider because the scent was almost cloying.

Fanny took them up to see Mrs Doulton as soon as they arrived; Judith felt her staring at Mrs Murry, Fanny was curious and, she suspected, slightly jealous. She was possessive towards Mrs Doulton, they had been together for years, they must have shared a thousand secrets, even if Mrs Doulton hadn't always realised how much of her life Fanny shared. The old woman couldn't have lived in the same house without finding out most of what went on, perhaps she had lived vicariously through Mrs Doulton, almost believing that she herself was part of that world. Judith sensed that Fanny preferred it when there were no visitors; she was old, she did not like strangers.

'What beautiful roses,' said Mrs Doulton as Mrs Murry laid them on the bedside table a moment later. 'I've been wanting to meet you for a long time; Judith has told me so much about you—it's very kind of you to come to see me, I hope the car journey wasn't too tiring.'

'Certainly not!' Mrs Murry said indignantly, bristling.

'Do sit down.'

Mrs Murry sat on the chair Judith hurriedly brought forward. 'You have a very charming house; have you lived here long?'

'I bought it after my husband died; I needed something to occupy my mind, I didn't want to spend all my time brooding and our home in the States held too many memories, I couldn't get over his death while I was there.'

'I couldn't bear to leave our home,' Mrs Murry explained. 'For that very reason—all the memories.'

'We all cope with it in a different way, I suppose. I felt I ought to go away, to leave Luke room—taking over from his father wasn't easy for him, he was still so young and most of the men he worked with were much more experienced. They kept trying to bring me in to support them, it made Luke feel that they were putting him down all the time, rubbing it in that he wasn't old enough to have control of the firm. It might have ruined our relationship if it had gone on much longer— I had to get out of the way.'

'You have daughters, too, don't you?'

'Two—did you have any daughters?' Mrs Doulton broke off to look at Judith who was fingering one of the roses. 'Oh, Judith, would you take those down to Fanny and ask her to put them in water for me? I wouldn't want them to wither.'

'Surely,' said Judith, getting up and gathering the roses into her crooked arm.

Mrs Doulton smiled at her. 'Why don't you go out and swim? Fanny will find you one of Angela's swimsuits to wear—it's such a lovely day, it seems a waste for you to spend it in here.' She looked at Mrs Murry. 'We can have a chat while we drink our coffee,' she added.

Judith went down the stairs, smiling to herself. There hadn't been room for her in that conversation, they had had too much to say to each other, but she felt she had been dismissed like a child from an adult chat, not hurtfully, because the dismissal had been given too kindly, but firmly. She had been sent out to play, they were going to discuss experiences she had not shared and could not quite understand. Fanny took the flowers from her and began to trim them before filling a green glass vase with water and putting the roses into it.

'Mrs Doulton said I could borrow one of Angela's bikinis,' Judith told her as she watched.

'Top drawer in her dressing-table,' Fanny said huffily. 'You can't miss them; there's nothing else in that drawer. You can get a towel from the bathroom airing cupboard.'

'Thank you,' Judith said politely, and left her to finish arranging the roses; she was doing so with rough impatience as though the velvety flowers were recalcitrant children she was hustling about.

Judith spent the rest of the time until lunch swimming in the blue-watered pool; a few white petals blew from the climbing roses which clung to a trellis nearby, she watched them floating on the top of the pool, it made her feel like someone in a film except that the petals gradually turned brown at the edges and began to sink. She was relieved to see no sign of Angela and her family; obviously they were going to be alone for lunch. When she got back to the house to her amazement Mrs Doulton was downstairs, sitting in a wheelchair in the sitting-room, talking to Judith's grandmother as they both sipped tiny glasses of sherry. Judith had never seen Mrs Doulton out of bed, she had supposed that Luke's mother was permanently bed-ridden, but when she asked about it Mrs Doulton laughed, shaking her head.

'Oh, no, I've only spent so much time in bed because of my operation. It wasn't a success and the pain was so bad that I couldn't face trying to walk far, but I'm finding it easier to move about lately. My doctor tells me I must make myself get up at least once daily, even if it's only to walk to the bathroom.' Mrs Doulton made a face. 'I'm a coward, I'm afraid. I hate pain.'

'Fanny and I helped her downstairs,' Mrs Murry told Judith. 'I've been telling her, she either ought to have a lift installed or sleep downstairs. When she's alone here Fanny wouldn't be able to get her downstairs.'

'In a few months I'm going to have another operation in the hope of getting it right this time,' Mrs Doulton said to Judith. 'I don't want to spend the rest of my life in a bed or a wheelchair—these hip operations are very delicate, but hundreds of people have had them successfully now, my doctor tells me. It was just bad luck that mine didn't quite come off.'

'I thought you said you were a coward,' Mrs Murry teased. 'It seems very brave of you to consider having another go.'

'Anything is better than lying about all day. The problem is that with a weak heart the doctors are reluctant to risk long operations, but they say they think they can do something.'

Judith felt a qualm of anxiety; she was already very fond of Luke's mother, she was frightened by the idea of her going into another major operation. Did Luke know what she planned? How would he feel about it?

They had lunch in the sunny dining-room; Fanny had placed the green glass vase of roses in the middle of the table, their perfume saturated the air and Mrs Doulton looked at them with pleasure. 'I love to be surrounded by flowers; one of the things I've missed most all these months has been my garden. I'm a great gardener, I was planning a water garden down in the park, but I haven't been able to get round to starting it because of my illness.'

'I love gardening,' Mrs Murry agreed. 'I haven't got room for a water garden, of course, but what an exciting project—what were you thinking of having? Lilies, irises . . .'

Judith watched a greenfinch pecking at the fruit on a cherry tree which grew not far from the dining-room window; the cherries were formed but unripe as yet, their white flesh must be very tart.

They drank their coffee in the sitting-room, Judith nursed her cup and listened while the other two women talked about gardens. They were obviously getting on very well, the conversation never flagged, they sometimes interrupted each other in their eagerness to agree, or argue against what the other was saying. Mrs Murry wasn't always easy to get on with, she could be rather sharp and obstinate, her prickly sense of pride often caused difficulties with other people, but Judith could see that she and Mrs Doulton spoke the same language, and Judith was delighted by this surprising friendship.

'I'll bring you a root of that,' Mrs Murry promised as they talked about a rock plant which Mrs Doulton did not know. 'It's originally from the Himalayas, you won't find it in a nursery unless you're lucky.' Mrs Murry's tone amused Judith; her grandmother's satisfaction in being able to give Mrs Doulton something was quite audible. It didn't surprise Judith; Mrs Murry hated to accept kindnesses unless she could repay them, that was why she had insisted on bringing the roses with her.

'You are kind,' Mrs Doulton said with reassuring gratitude. 'I'd love to have a root of it—I wonder how it will transplant? Our earth must be much richer than yours, do you think it likes a more acid soil?'

Judith switched off; she was no gardener. Surreptitiously she glanced at the clock, it was gone three and she must suggest leaving soon.

Mrs Doulton stopped talking, her head to one side in an attitude that reminded Judith of a missel thrush on the lawns around the house, listening for worms. 'Now who is that?' she murmured. 'Did you hear a car or am I imagining it?'

Mrs Murry listened, too. 'I do hear voices,' she said, and Judith stiffened, her cup rocking in its saucer. She held her hand steady, listening intently. Yes, she could hear Luke's voice. She had known it; hadn't she known he would arrive? He must have flown back from Paris this afternoon. Why had he come down here? But then she heard Baba laughing and her colour drained away. Baba was back. She was back and Luke had brought her down here to see his mother. He wouldn't do that if he wasn't happy to go through with the marriage. Judith's emotions collided inside her like a train crash; anger, pain, humiliation, resentment all toppled one on the other.

The door opened and Baba smiled at them all. 'Hallo, surprise, surprise!' She was wearing a very chic powder blue dress with a matching jacket cut to hug her small waist; she looked terrific, but then she always looked terrific, there was nothing new about that. She was talking vivaciously as she walked in with Luke at her shoulder. 'Isn't this weather gorgeous? I was afraid it would be pouring with rain when I got back to Heathrow. This is super!'

'How did you like California, Baba?' Mrs Doulton asked.

'Oh, fabulous—I'm really sold on it, I hated to leave.'

'We have a nice house in Vermont, I'm sure you'll like that, too,' Mrs Doulton said, and Luke gave her a wry smile. He hadn't looked at Judith, he was wearing an expression she found difficult to read, the only word she could think of to describe it was wary. Luke looked like a man very carefully watching where he put his feet; she wasn't sure what that meant.

'I'm afraid Baba wouldn't think much of Vermont—

there isn't a big department store within fifty miles and it rains too often.'

'Oh, Luke, don't tease,' said Baba, tossing her hair back and laughing.

Judith switched off. She did not want to hear any of this, and so she missed the moment when her grandmother suggested taking Mrs Doulton for a walk around the garden. The first Judith knew of what was being discussed was when Luke pushed his mother out of the room with Mrs Murry hurrying ahead; Judith looked up and Baba sat down next to her on the sofa and gave her a suddenly nervous smile.

'I wish Luke hadn't brought me here this afternoon— I want to talk to him, but I can't decide what to say and this isn't the place we can talk, anyway. I went to see him at the minute I landed at Heathrow and he was just about to leave to come here, so he said: come on with me. So I came.' Baba made a little face, half laughing, half worried. 'I don't know what to do, Judith, that's the truth.'

'About what?' Judith asked with reluctance. She did not want to discuss Luke with Baba, but she couldn't think of a way of stopping Baba without being rude.

Baba looked at her, then at the door. They heard Luke talking at the front door. Baba lowered her voice. 'Well ... it isn't official yet, but ...' Suddenly her whole face lit up and Judith saw that she was luminous with excitement behind her smile. 'I've got the part!'

'Congratulations,' said Judith, trying to sound as happy as Baba was. 'That's wonderful! I'm so pleased for you.'

'I've been hanging on over there because Joey, the director making the film, said he was sure he could talk the producer round, he wanted me there so that I'd be on hand whenever the producer came to see him. It was nerve-racking, Judith; I thought I'd bite my nails down to the fingers! But yesterday morning the producer said okay, I could do the film. He couldn't get anyone else, you see; I was the only one halfway suitable and my only drawback was that I was unknown.'

Judith listened as Baba talked on and on about the film, Beverly Hills, the director and his wife, who had become a close friend, the wonderful life style they had and how much Baba had loved it all.

'Have you told Luke?' asked Judith, and Baba stopped smiling and shook her head, her eyes worried.

'I don't know how to break it to him. If you were me, Judith, what would you do? I can't bear to give up this part—but then there's Luke ... I won't see much of him for ages. Most of the film is being shot in the studios; I'll have to live in Beverly Hills. I'll get an apartment, my agent's over the moon about how much I'll be earning. I'm moving into a new income bracket entirely.' Baba stopped as Judith moved restlessly. Baba kept getting away from the point at which she held Judith's interest; she was too excited about the film to be able to keep her mind on the subject of Luke, and that was all that interested Judith. Baba gave her a helpless, pleading look, her big blue eyes wide. 'Oh, Judith, what am I going to do about Luke? The idea of getting married at the moment is out—we'll have to postpone it for at least a year. My agent can't make up his mind whether it's good publicity or not—Luke's big news, of course, but it might be better if I was free.' Baba smiled to herself and Judith wondered why, then Baba said: 'What would you do if you were me, Judith?' again and Judith felt like hitting her.

'Don't ask me!' she said coolly. 'You must make up your own mind—it's your life.'

'Of course, I'm mad about Luke,' said Baba, but the statement didn't ring true, not any more Judith looked at her with disbelief. 'He's absolutely fabulous and I want to marry him, but I couldn't bear to give up the film—I've got to think about my career. If everything worked out, I could be a big star in a year's time! I'm absolutely torn, Judith darling.' She gave Judith a tragic look and Judith wondered if she was rehearsing a big scene from the film. 'What do you do when your heart tells you to go one way and your head tells you to go another?' Baba asked her, and Judith was very tempted to scream.

'I'm not involved,' she said with great restraint. 'It isn't my problem, it's yours. Don't drag me into it.' She wanted to yell: you phoney! at her. She had been taken in by Baba's sweet good nature and sunny smile for years, and now she saw a new Baba, a girl who was ditching the man she claimed she loved because she preferred her career. When Baba first told her that she was keeping the chance of a part in a film from Luke, Judith had been surprised, now she saw that it was part and parcel of the whole thing. Baba liked life smooth and knot-free; when she ran up against a knot she just went round it any way she could and if she had to lie, or break an engagement, in the process—well, that was tough, but she did it with a smile and a sigh and a pleading look in those big blue eyes. Baba used her yielding look of femininity with ruthless awareness of what it could do, why hadn't she seen that before? Because Baba hadn't operated in quite that way when she was around until now? If Judith had ever known any of Baba's ex-boyfriends she might have seen a very different image, she suspected. She had often wondered about the way Baba's men came and went with such rapidity; Baba had usually explained to Ruth that their intentions were not precisely honourable, but maybe that had not been the whole truth. Maybe it had been Baba whose intentions were suspect.

'I've been trying to get up the nerve to tell him all the

way down here,' Baba confided. 'Luke can be a bit scarey, you know, Judith. I'm not sure how he'll react; what shall I say to him?'

'I'm sure you'll think of something,' Judith said drily.

'I'm only being practical,' Baba protested, picking up the hint of criticism Judith could not quite suppress. 'If I went through with the wedding I'd hardly see him for months. That's no way to start a marriage.'

'I don't know why you're telling me—tell Luke. Or do you need a rehearsal?'

Baba looked at her, open-eyed in shocked surprise. 'Judith! That's not very kind. You sound quite nasty.'

'Do I? Gracious, sorry,' said Judith, getting up. 'I'll go and join the others. Shall I send Luke to you?'

As she got up, Baba caught at her hand, her golden head flung back and her mouth quivering. It was, Judith thought, a rather hammy performance. 'Oh, Judith, I can't bear to tell him, he'll be so angry and hurt—I thought . . . couldn't you . . .'

'No, I damned well couldn't!' Judith snapped furiously, and walked out before she really lost her temper. She had been putting herself through hell because of a misguided sense of loyalty to Baba, and all the time Baba had been having a terrific time in Hollywood and had come back determined to jilt Luke anyway. Judith had a dark suspicion that she had met someone else over there; she had caught a secretive, complacent smile now and then which looked very much like the smile a woman gives, thinking about a man.

She found Luke on the drive, his back to her, his hands in his tweed jacket pockets as he watched a magpie flap across the clear summer sky.

'One for sorrow,' Judith thought aloud, and he half turned to look at her, his mouth wry.

'There's another one over there in the elm—I think they're nesting here.'

'Two for joy, then,' Judith said lightly. 'Baba wants you.' As she heard how she had phrased it she wished she could recall the sentence. Baba did not want him, but Judith did, but she would have died rather than let Baba see that.

Luke's mouth compressed, he nodded, turning towards the house. Judith walked towards the low box hedges surrounding neat flower beds; she saw her grandmother pushing Mrs Doulton's wheelchair towards one of the yew bushes trimmed into peacocks. At close quarters the tail looked a little ragged. Judith heard the two women laughing at it.

'More like a chicken,' Mrs Murry observed.

'I've never like peacocks, anyway—vain, hysterical birds and very bad-tempered,' Mrs Doulton agreed.

They looked round as Judith joined them. 'I'm afraid we ought to be going soon,' Judith said.

'Must you? I have enjoyed this afternoon,' said Mrs Doulton. 'It's the first time I've been out of the house for months—how lucky that the weather was so good.'

They walked back to the house slowly and Fanny helped to wheel Mrs Doulton inside, her expression gloomy. 'I hope you haven't caught a chill out there. You should have worn something warmer than that jacket. You ought to have had a blanket around you.'

'Don't fuss!' Mrs Doulton protested.

'We must go,' Judith insisted and her grandmother put on the jacket Fanny brought to her.

'Fetch Luke,' Mrs Doulton suggested, and Judith said quickly that he was talking to Baba and there was no need to disturb them, she would be seeing him in the office next day anyway.

'Don't forget that root,' Mrs Doulton told Mrs Murry. 'Judith must bring you down again soon.'

Judith couldn't wait to get away; she wondered how Luke was taking Baba's news. He had said he wanted to get out of the engagement, but he was a very masculine man, how would his ego react to discovering that Baba was jilting him, rather than the other way around? As she drove back to London her mind dwelt continually on Luke's reactions; it was stupid to speculate without knowing what Baba was actually telling him. Judith was afraid to be too happy, she couldn't quite believe that Luke was going to be free so easily, but she could not have borne to wait to see his face afterwards. She was afraid. Now that he had seen Baba again, been reminded of how beautiful she was, been able to see Judith next to her and be forcibly made aware that Judith was very far from beautiful—how would he feel on being immediately told that Baba did not want to marry him?

After all, he had chosen Baba in the first place because of her beauty. In spite of having told Judith that he loved her and didn't care whether she was attractive or not, she couldn't feel over-confident about Luke's feelings. While Baba was out of sight she had believed he loved her. Now that Baba was back she had painful doubts again; about herself, about Luke. Baba had always been able to make Judith feel very plain. She could remember as a teenager standing in Ruth's bedroom listening to Baba as she looked into the mirror with a happy smile. 'How do I loko, Judith? Do you think this colour suits me? Is my hair okay?' Baba had always asked you questions to which she knew the answer, she only asked because she enjoyed hearing you tell her she looked fantastic. Judith had avoided the mirror; she did not want Baba to look at her and then say very kindly: 'That isn't quite your colour, that's all, Judith. What a pity you're so skinny, you've hardly got a bust at all, but never mind, nobody will notice.' They will be looking at *me*! Baba's face had added silently.

Baba hadn't been spiteful, her sweetness had been

false, that was all. She had always been looking into mirrors, enjoying the image of herself they gave her back. No doubt she would be perfectly at home in the mirror world of the cinema.

Judith dropped her grandmother and then drove on to her flat. It was almost six-thirty and there was nothing on television but the news and the religious programmes following it. She had a bath at seven, got herself a boiled egg and some toast and settled down to read a fat paperback which she had had around for weeks without opening. She was pampering herself tonight; for weeks she had been working flat out and she deserved some relaxation. By eight o'clock it was almost dark. She switched on the lights and drew the curtains, curling up on a couch with the book and a pillow behind her head. She would go to bed early; in an hour, probably.

The book was printed on yellowish paper which made it hard to read, the print was far too small, there were too many pages. Judith's mind kept straying back to Luke. Was the engagement over now? Was he free? Or had he talked Baba out of jilting him? Given the choice between herself and a girl like Baba, what man could prefer her? Perhaps he had realised as soon as he saw Baba again that what he had thought he felt for Judith had been merely infatuation. They had been flung together during the past month, Baba had been out of sight, Luke might have drifted into imagining that he was in love.

She looked at her watch; she couldn't go to bed yet. The book was boring her to tears but she went on reading it, it was better than sitting there thinking about Luke all the time. She lifted her head, listening to the silence. What are you waiting for? she asked herself irritably. He won't come.

That was what she was waiting for—for Luke. If

Baba had set him free and he really loved her, he would come to her.

If he didn't come, he didn't love her after all. She forced herself back to her book. She wouldn't think about that yet. Time enough when she knew that Luke had chosen Baba. There would be plenty of time in the future for her to cry then; she wasn't running to meet the anguish which that realisation would bring. She was waiting. She looked at her watch again. Ten minutes had passed. It felt like ten years. She almost went to the mirror to look for grey hairs, she felt as though she must have acquired some.

Her intelligence said: you could have fought for him. You could have given Baba the approval she wanted, told her you didn't blame her, advised her to go after a career and forget Luke. She closed her eyes. If she had agreed to tell Luke what Baba wanted her to tell him she could have got Luke on the rebound there and then. She had walked away and made Baba do her own dirty work, and maybe that had been a fatal mistake because you could never guess what will happen between two people, especially when sex is mixed up in it.

But she knew she couldn't have acted any other way, her own integrity wouldn't have permitted it. The very fact that she had been sick with happiness at the news that Baba didn't want to marry Luke after all had made it obvious that she must stay out of it. It had been between Luke and Baba and none of her business. They had made that engagement, they must unmake it.

She put down her book and went slowly into the kitchen to make herself some coffee. It was nearly ten o'clock. Luke hadn't come, he wasn't going to come, and she could feel the remorseless tread of pain coming nearer as she waited and realised that she had lost.

The doorbell rang and her whole body jerked in

shock. She slowly put down the cup of coffee, slowly walked to the door. It could be a neighbour asking to borrow a cup of sugar, or a policeman telling her that she had parked without leaving on her lights. She coolly warned herself of disappointment before she opened the door.

Luke walked in and looked down at her; his grey eyes were brilliant in the dim light of the little hall. Judith closed the door and stood there, trembling. She couldn't say a thing.

'You know. She said she'd told you,' Luke said.

Judith swallowed, she was still waiting, she could not believe that she was going to be so happy, it did not seem possible.

'Why did you run away like that, then?' Luke demanded harshly, staring down at her, so close that she could see the little golden flecks ringing the iris of his eyes.

'I wasn't running away, I was driving my grand-mother home.'

'You must have known I'd come to look for you after I'd talked to Baba.'

'I didn't know what you'd do,' said Judith, and his grey eyes flashed with sudden anger.

'You didn't know?' There was violence in his face, she thought for a second he was going to hit her, then he turned and walked into the sitting-room and she followed slowly. He sat down on the couch, his body tense. Judith stood there, uneasily watching him.

'I love you,' he said to his shoes. 'But I sometimes wonder why. I can never quite work out your reasons for doing anything. You knew I didn't want to marry Baba. You knew I was in love with you. From the minute she arrived today I've been trying to tell her I couldn't marry her, that I'd made a terrible mistake—when she told me first I was speechless. I had a hard time not grinning from ear to ear. But I managed to be polite and say I didn't blame her, she was probably going to be another Marilyn Monroe and I wished her all the luck in the world. Then I went to look for you, but you'd gone and I couldn't work out why. So I drove Baba home and said goodbye and told her to keep the ring, which she was quite happy to do.' Judith caught the glint of derision with which he said that. Was he secretly angry with Baba? 'I thought of coming straight here, but I needed to think out why you'd rushed off without even saying goodbye, so I went and had a few drinks,' he said.

'Oh, did you?' Judith said warily; was that what made his eyes so brilliant?

He looked up then. 'I'm not drunk,' he said with aggression.

'I didn't think you were.'

'You sounded as though you did. Why did you go, Judith? Why?'

'I wanted to leave you room,' she said, remembering what his mother had said to her and her grandmother earlier that day. 'You don't have to feel obliged to . . .'

'Shut up!' Luke muttered explosively. He lunged forward and grabbed her wrist, jerked her across his lap and kissed her with passion and a reined ferocity. Her mouth trembled for a second at the heat and fury in the kiss, then she let her arms go round his neck and kissed him back softly, her lips parting to admit him.

He lifted his head later, breathing sharply. 'I've been dying to kiss you for days, you know that; it's been torture not touching you—how could you do that to us, Judith? Seeing you every day, having to keep my distance—it was more than flesh and blood could stand. I haven't been sleeping; when I did manage to get to sleep I dreamed about you. I've been so frustrated it's a wonder I've managed to stay sane.'

'I couldn't steal you from Baba,' she explained, her fingertips caressing the smooth brown skin of his throat. She undid his tie while he watched, one brow arching slightly in silent comment. Judith dropped the tie to the floor and began to undo his shirt.

'I thought I was going to have a hell of a scene on my hands when I told her,' said Luke, shrugging out of his jacket. It wasn't easy with Judith on his lap, it made her laugh and he looked at her with lighthearted amusement.

'I hope you never regret it after she's become a sex symbol for the eighties,' said Judith, her palm sliding down the muscular line of his chest.

'I'll be able to boast that I was the one who got away,' smiled Luke, tugging her shirt out of her waistband.

'Don't tear that, it's pure silk,' Judith protested, and slid out of the shirt before he damaged it.

Luke looked down at her slender body in the lemon silk slip, she heard him breathing with shallow irregularity. 'I've been waiting to get you into bed for what seems years.' His cool fingers slowly pulled down the straps on the slip and then he undid her bra with what she felt was far too practised a technique.

'You've done this before,' she reproached.

'Have you?' He bent his head and she took a fierce breath as his lips brushed lightly over the nipple of one breast. 'Judith ...' She felt his hands moving over her warm skin and a soft cry broke out of her at the pleasure of what he was doing. Heat was growing inside her, inside both of them, and she watched him with intense passion as he lifted his head. His face was darkly flushed; she felt like someone who has been struggling with a heavy load up a hill and then suddenly finds herself after a bitter time, running down hill unable to stop. 'This isn't where we should be,' whispered Luke, and he shifted her sideways and got up. He picked her up and walked towards the bedroom.

'I love you,' Judith whispered, her face half buried in his neck where his blood beat fiercely under the warm skin. 'I wish I was beautiful for you . . .'

'I've never seen anything so beautiful in my life,' said Luke as he put her down on the bed, and as his body came down to join her she arched to meet it.

A WORD ABOUT THE AUTHOR

Since she began writing for Harlequin Presents in late 1978, Charlotte Lamb has had close to forty books in this series published. Her explanation for this tremendous volume of superb romance writing is simple: "I love to write, and it comes very easily to me."

Once Charlotte has begun a story, the plot, the actions and the personalities of the characters unfold effortlessly and spontaneously, as her quick fingers commit the ideas of her fertile imagination to paper.

And so, in her beautiful old home on the rain-swept, uncrowded Isle of Man, where she lives with her husband and five children, Charlotte spends eight hours a day at her typewriter spinning loves stories — and enjoying every minute of it!

Her career as a writer has opened many doors for her, and travel is one of them. Yet despite all the countries she has visited and enjoyed in the past few years, her greatest love is still London, the city where she was born and raised.

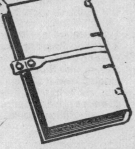